David and Bathsheba

Through Nathan's Eyes

Joel Cohen

HiddenSpring

Jacket design by Cynthia Dunne
Book design by Lynn Else

Library of Congress Cataloging-in-Publication Data

Cohen, Joel, 1944–
David and Bathsheba : through Nathan's eyes / Joel Cohen.
    p. cm.
    Summary: A first-person fictional account of the sin of David and Bathsheba through the eyes of the prophet Nathan.
    ISBN 978-1-58768-041-0 (cloth : alk. paper)
    1. David, King of Israel—Fiction. 2. Bathsheba (Biblical figure)—Fiction.
3. Nathan (Biblical prophet)—Fiction. 4. Israel—Kings and rulers—Fiction.
5. Women in the Bible—Fiction. I. Title.
    PS3603.O364D38 2007
    813'.6—dc22

2007002835

Published by HiddenSpring
an imprint of Paulist Press
997 Macarthur Boulevard
Mahwah, New Jersey 07430

www.hiddenspringbooks.com

Printed and bound in the United States of America

To the memory of
Nathan Cohen, who grasped the
"responsibility" of condemning wrong—
whose character reflected the integrity
of his namesake

And Samuel said to Saul, "…but now your kingdom will not continue; the LORD has sought out a man [David] after his own heart; and the LORD has appointed him to be ruler over his people, because you have not kept what the LORD commanded you."   1 Samuel 13:13–14

When he had removed [Saul], he made David their king. In his testimony about him he said, "I have found David, son of Jesse, to be a man after my heart, who will carry out all my wishes." Of this man's posterity God has brought to Israel a Savior, Jesus, as he promised….
Acts 13:22–23

Afterward the Israelites shall return and seek the LORD their God, and David their king; they shall come in awe to the LORD and to his goodness in the latter days.
Hosea 3:5

Contents

Preface

S peak truth to power" is an evocative phrase that entered our contemporary political vocabulary through the Quaker tradition, but the idea begins in the Hebrew Bible, where the men and women we know as prophets are shown to confront and condemn the most powerful kings and emperors of the ancient world. The archetype is Moses in the court of Pharaoh, of course, but perhaps the single most poignant example is the remarkable encounter between King David and the man called Nathan.

David is a celebrated figure in the Bible and in the traditions of both Judaism and Christianity. His name appears more than a thousand times in the Hebrew Bible, his exploits can be detected in passages where his name is not mentioned at all, and his memory is kept alive in the messianic expectations of both faiths. Indeed, an argument can be made (and has been made) that the composition of the biblical text began with a biography of David and grew by accretion as later writings were added to the narrative in the Book of Samuel that scholars called the Court History of David.

By contrast, Nathan is obscure and overlooked. Ironically, as Joel Cohen aptly points out in the pages that follow, no book in the Bible bears his name. And yet Nathan is also a decisive character in the biblical saga, not only in the life of David but in the moral imperative that makes the Bible a sacred text rather than a book of history or biography. David himself is redeemed from his own all-too-human faults and failings only by the admonishment and instruction that he receives from Nathan. Without Nathan, we might conclude, David may have been a great man but not a good one.

Above all, the encounter between David and Nathan, so expertly and touchingly evoked by the author of this book, can be seen as the flashpoint between the sacred and the secular. Much of what David is shown to do in the Bible is scandalous and shocking—"the kind of details," according to Bible scholar Peter Ackroyd, "for which, in our more sophisticated times, the Sunday newspapers of the slightly less reputable kind pay handsomely." And yet, like David himself, generation after generation of Bible readers have been compelled by Nathan to make some kind of moral sense out of it all.

Exactly here we find what may be regarded as one of the "gifts of the Jews," according to Thomas Cahill's felicitous phrase. Countless other faiths that came before and after Judaism know both kings and priests; indeed, the unsettled relationship between secular and religious authority is one of the great engines of history, no less in our own troubled world than in distant biblical antiquity. But the Bible adds a third player to the drama—the otherwise ordinary man or woman, lacking rank or title but blessed with a fiery conscience and a gifted tongue, who is inspired to address even a king in the name of God.

Jonathan Kirsch

Introduction

The prophets of Israel were God's instrumentalities on earth to tell Israel what it needed to hear. Oftentimes, the Word they imparted was not easy, for they spoke, albeit and typically in metaphor, of the wages of sin—the harsh and unforgiving wages of sin. When they spoke, they spoke to the sinfulness of the entire House of Israel.

Not so the Prophet Nathan. Although the Book of Chronicles tells us that there was once one, no Book has survived that bears his name. Still, we know that Nathan, unlike the other prophets in the Sacred Writings, spoke directly to only one man, describing the wages of that man's personal sin, not Israel's communal sin. He told King David, the sinner, of the punishment that would befall him for his carnal sin with Bathsheba and the intended death of her husband Uriah—that his infant son would die in innocence. And because the Prophet brought King David to condemn himself and almost in an instant the prophecy came true, the Prophet spoke to all Israel. And all of its House has listened to his simple parable ever since.

If there still were a Book of Nathan, perhaps we might know more of the man who was appointed by God to face the mighty King David and boldly tell him, as would no other man: "You are a sinner!" We might have come to know that God chose him for the role because of his integrity, or his bravery, or the standing he held in the King's Court. Or that he was chosen precisely because he "lacked" all of those characteristics—poetic irony, since David was chosen by God to bring forth the Messiah despite his sinfulness. But we are left without an answer. All we have is that God told Nathan what to do and he did it, with discipline and integrity!

We will never know if, when Nathan condemned the King of Israel, the forebear of the Messiah, the Prophet coarsely pressed his finger to the warrior's chest, or spoke to the King in discreet privacy—whether tears rolled down the Prophet's cheek when he spoke, or whether Nathan was so repulsed by the sinful conduct of David that he simply "pronounced sentence" on the King, and turned his back to walk away.

As is always true in capturing the meaning of biblical narrative, only the human imagination can be invoked to suppose what actually transpired beyond the sparse words delegated in the text—and no one man's imagination is better than another's in furnishing, for him, that which remains unstated. And, today, when we live in a diaspora from "authoritativeness," man's attempts to interpret the Bible are "unauthorized," except for the truth that one's imagination, if you believe in Him, is "God-given."

What follows, then, is the imagination (or conjecture) of just one man, the writer—drawn to the undertaking by the meaningfulness of this biblical story, and the character of one man who lived in the Prophet Nathan's credo.

Abbreviations

BaR	Medresh B'midbar Rabah
BHM	Bais Medresh
ER	Seder Eliahu Rabah VeSeder Eliahu
Hal.	Halacha
PR	Medresh Pisikta Rabosi
PRE	Pirkie Rabbi Eleazar

The Story

In ancient times, in the days of King Saul, the Philistine giant Goliath challenged the Children of Israel with extinction. A youthful David, son of Jesse, a shepherd boy, emerged. Overcoming odds of great moment, he killed the giant, gaining the hero worship of all of Israel. Years later when Saul was defeated in battle, David was anointed King of Israel. He thrived as a gifted king, warrior, and psalmist—the progenitor of the Messiah. When the King implored God to let him build the Temple, the Prophet Nathan was dispatched by God to tell him that it was not to be. The King beckoned God to change His mind—imploring God to test him to prove his worthiness. And God so tested him.

One day, in a season when kings should be away to war, David remained at the Palace in Jerusalem. Standing on his rooftop, he was struck by the beauty of Bathsheba, wife of his soldier—Uriah the Hittite. Overcome by his lust, David demanded that she be delivered to him, and he lay with her. David failed God's test. When she later sent him word of her pregnancy, he tried to trick Uriah into believing it was his child. Failing to persuade the furloughed Uriah, who longed to return to battle, to return to his wife, the King chose another strategy. David directed Uriah to deliver a sealed message to his general at the battlefront that Uriah should be sent to the frontlines and abandoned, left to be killed by the enemy. The sword of the enemy felled Uriah.

When Bathsheba's time of mourning for Uriah passed, David wed her; a baby boy, come from their adulterous encounter, was later born.

The Lord was gravely displeased with David for his sin. He sent the Prophet Nathan to confront the King. Using a ploy to cause David to unwittingly condemn himself, Nathan told the King that "the sword shall never depart from your house." The Prophet's words were piercing: David and Bathsheba would be spared, but the baby born of their union would die seven days later in his innocence. Soon, the prophecy would come to pass: the arrogance of asking for God's test.

1

The Death of the Baby

Then Nathan went to his house. The Lord struck the child that Uriah's wife bore to David, and it became very ill. David therefore pleaded with God for the child; David fasted, and went in and lay all night on the ground. The elders of his house stood beside him, urging him to rise from the ground; but he would not, nor did he eat food with them. On the seventh day the child died. And the servants of David were afraid to tell him that the child was dead; for they said, "While the child was still alive, we spoke to him, and he did not listen to us; how then can we tell him the child is dead? He may do himself some harm." But when David saw that his servants were whispering together, he perceived that the child was dead; and David said to his servants, "Is the child dead?" They said, "He is dead." Then David rose from the ground, washed, anointed himself, and changed his clothes. He went into the house of the Lord, and worshiped; he then went to his own house; and when he asked, they set food before him and he ate. Then his servants said to him, "What is this thing that you have done? You fasted and wept for the child while it was alive; but when the child died, you rose and ate food." He said, "While the child was still alive, I fasted and wept; for I said, 'Who knows? The Lord may be gracious to me, and the child may live.' But now he is dead; why should I fast? Can I bring him back again? I shall go to him, but he will not return to me."

(2 Samuel 12:15–23)

Thus says the LORD: A voice is heard in Ramah, lamentation and bitter weeping. Rachel is weeping for her children; she refuses to be comforted for her children, because they are no more. Thus says the LORD: Keep your voice from weeping, and your eyes from tears; for there is a reward for your work, says the LORD: they shall come back from the land of the enemy; there is hope for your future, says the LORD: your children shall come back to their own country. Indeed I heard Ephraim pleading: "You disciplined me, and I took the discipline; I was like a calf untrained. Bring me back, let me come back, for you are the LORD my God. For after I had turned away I repented; and after I was discovered, I struck my thigh; I was ashamed, and I was dismayed because I bore the disgrace of my youth." Is Ephraim my dear son? Is he the child I delight in? As often as I speak against him, I still remember him. Therefore I am deeply moved for him; I will surely have mercy on him, says the LORD.   (Jeremiah 31:15–20)

An innocent baby was buried one week ago before all of Israel.

The Death of the Baby

His father had slept on the ground and fasted for seven days as death engripped the infant. His servants stood over him to raise him from the ground, but he refused to arise and would not break bread with them. When he learned, however, that the baby was dead, he arose from the ground; he washed, anointed himself, and changed his garments, and came to the House of God and prostrated himself. He returned to his home and asked that he be served bread, and he ate. Confronted by his servants over why he had acted in this way despite the baby's death, he told them: Until that day, he thought, *"Who knows? The Lord may be gracious to me, and the child may live.' But now he is dead; why should I fast? Can I bring him back again? I shall go to him, but he will not return to me."*[1]

Nathan Descends the Palace Steps

Seven days ago, when the sun still stood high in the sky, I passed through a man's doors. As I left, they were shut coldly against my back by his obsequious servants. The man's tears still rolled down his cheeks. Their tracks betrayed him to the multitudes—revealing the wrenching anguish he so urgently tried to obscure from me.

I had just told the man that his son, recently born, would die while still a suckling baby. The baby was born innocent, but yet is destined for death—the ordinance of an unalterable death born in the lustful act of his father.

---

1. 2 Samuel 12:22–23.

That decree by me of the worst of what a man can be asked to endure, a prophetic vision given to me alone by God, is my life's lot—the only act for which I will ever be remembered. But do I show vanity in even considering how mankind will see my role in this, when God has simply commanded me to perform His role? I will be "celebrated" as the only man who could tell another, with certainty, not as a metaphor but as a fact, that *"your* sin, *your* sin alone, will cause the death of your baby." And that there will be no chance for you to reverse the decree.

As I descended the palace steps, my back was ramrod straight. But my stance was an artifice I employed to deceive the masses, maybe even myself. I had been ordained by God to decree to a man most powerful that, while he, himself, and his now-wife, will live despite his sin, his son, instead, will die for it—that *"the sword shall never depart from your house."* I did not feel the rectitude that my posture suggested.

The rude, unyielding glances from the King's acolytes that I had to chillingly endure that day, told me, without a word that needed to be uttered, that *David* composed the praises of God. *David* routed the Philistines. The son of David will build the Temple. *David's* loins will give life to the Messiah. There are those, even today in the face of his sin so ignominious, who say, as all the world will one day say of David, that *"if the Messiah-King comes from among the living, David will be his name…[a]nd if he comes from among the dead it will be David himself."*[2] The

---

2. Jerusalem Berakoth, Chap. 2, Hal. I. See J. Klausner, *The Messianic Idea in Israel* (London: George Allen & Unwin Ltd., 1956); J. Kirsch, *King David: The Real Life of the Man Who Ruled Israel* (New York: Ballantine Books, 2000).

Head of David, Michelangelo

"Fellow Israelites, I may say to you confidently of our ancestor David that he both died and was buried, and his tomb is with us to this day. Since he was a prophet, he knew that God had sworn with an oath to him that he would put one of his descendants on his throne. Foreseeing this, David spoke of the resurrection of the Messiah, saying, 'He was not abandoned to Hades, nor did his flesh experience corruption.' This Jesus God raised up, and of that all of us are witnesses. Being therefore exalted at the right hand of God, and having received from the Father the promise of the Holy Spirit, he has poured out this that you both see and hear. For David did not ascend into the heavens, but he himself says, 'The Lord said to my

mortal David, great as he is in life, will be eclipsed by the spectral David. Indeed, the belief that posits the spectral David will always bar me from the judgments I might properly make of any other mortal. Beliefs in matters of the Messiah are nothing less than reality.

And who is he who dared condemn David? Just a wrinkled man dressed as a beggar. He is a man who arrogantly pointed his finger to the King's chest and told the King, who might so easily have killed him as he did Goliath, Uriah the Hittite, and so many others, that the King is an adulterer and murderer: the King anointed for greatness by God Himself is an adulterer and murderer! Why must *I* be that man? Why must *I* be that prophet of doom? And is it not sinful for me to question God's direction of my life?

With all that David has and will have brought to the world, what did I bring but the prophecy of an innocent's death? Oh yes, I "see," too, that though the Temple will be built one day, in the days that will follow grooms will break a glass at their wedding ceremony to remember always that the Temple will also have been destroyed. *My* visions! Why must these visions be placed in *my* eyes? And, again, do *I* sin to quarrel with God's plan for me?

The Death of the Baby

Who am I to hold this seemingly satanic power to foretell death, and yet inwardly pray to God that I do not—that what I had just told the King of Israel will not, in the end, turn out true: that I spoke merely in folly. I wanted so badly to be *that* wrinkled beggarman; but one who has no such vision. But, yet, at that very moment one week ago, I did!

Lord, "Sit at my right hand, until I make your enemies your footstool." Therefore let the entire house of Israel know with certainty that God has made him both Lord and Messiah, this Jesus whom you crucified." (Acts 2:29–36)

How did I emerge that day from such obscurity—unlike the prophets who came before me, the patriarchs, or Moses or Samuel, who came to their stations of prophecy from uncommon greatness? Unlike them, the Scriptures never spoke of me before the events of one week ago, except to state the Lord's command to him that not King David, but after his death, his son, would build the Temple of God.

Where did this all start for me? I broke no idols of my father, as did Abraham. I had no sister who prophesied my place as the Redeemer, as did Moses. No mother of mine, as Samuel's, beckoned the Lord in torment over a closed womb. I was no hero youth as was the prophet-king I was called upon to rebuke. Can just an ordinary man like me stand stridently in the face of the Messiah's forebearer, David, son of Jesse?

Surely, God had come to me in yester-nights. And I had dialogue with the King on the morrows of those nighttimes gone by. Each time the King warmly greeted me, as he did the Prophet Samuel before me, and listened patiently to what, in vision, God had imparted to me in those exquisite night visits I had from God.

"[Hannah] made this vow: "O LORD of hosts, if only you…remember me…but will give to your servant a male child, then I will set him before you as a nazirite…." (1 Samuel 1:11)

But the King himself is a prophet (although, for some reason, God never spoke to him as He has me). Did he not himself already "know" what I could tell him of the future? Ever the skillful warrior, perhaps he believed that I could tell him that if he sent his soldiers into battle hither they would be slaughtered, but would remain safe if otherwise. But that power to see the future was denied both him and me. I had no such insight into immediacy until a week ago—and my recent insight, from just days ago, offers no possibility of *saving* life!

What a prophet knows, he need not have learned from a nighttime visit from the Almighty. God had instructed me to hold my ears to the ground—men who hold the title "Man of God" must know the worldly itself to best perceive the Otherworldly.

2

The Temptation of David

In the spring of the year, the time when kings go out to battle, David sent Joab with his officers and all Israel with him; they ravaged the Ammonites, and besieged Rabbah. But David remained at Jerusalem. It happened, late one afternoon, when David rose from his couch and was walking about on the roof of the king's house, that he saw from the roof a woman bathing; the woman was very beautiful. David sent someone to inquire about the woman. It was reported, "This is Bathsheba daughter of Eliam, the wife of Uriah the Hittite." So David sent messengers to get her, and she came to him, and he lay with her. (Now she was purifying herself after her period.) Then she returned to her house. The woman conceived; and she sent and told David, "I am pregnant." (2 Samuel 11:1–5)

It was no secret that King David was a lustful man—perhaps the *persona* of an able warrior must seek out conquest even in days of peace. And the eventide that brought upon King David's moral downfall was at a season when he should have been away at battle against the Children of Ammon. But for reasons still obscure to me, he stayed behind whilst only his generals and soldiers faced battle. He stayed back and undertook a conquest

"It interested Joab to analyze the character of men and their opinions. When he heard King David's words: 'Like as a father pitieth his children, so the LORD pitieth them that fear him,' he expressed his astonishment that the comparison should be made with the love of a father for a child, and not with the love of a mother; mother love as a rule is *considered* the stronger and the more self-sacrificing. He made up his mind to keep his eyes open, and observe whether David's idea was borne out by facts."
(The Legends of the Jews, IV, pp. 97–98)

"Joab exclaimed: 'Yes, David was right when he *compared* God's love for men to a father's love for his child.'"
(The Legends of the Jews, IV, p. 98)

of another sort, a woman who promiscuously and openly bathed on a rooftop terrace nearby the Palace. The women he already had taken to his chamber in the sacrosanctity of marriage were not nearly enough for the King: the appalling outcome of a custom that authorizes polygamy!

No, the voluptuous Bathsheba, who would one day become the one and true love of his life, was what he frantically desired; and though he learned from his servants that she was married to Uriah the Hittite, a soldier in the King's army off at war, he demanded that she be brought to him to satisfy his urging for her. And he sinfully lay with her with full knowledge of his servants who had taken her to him; I knew this—God's nighttime visions are only there to bring the future, not the past. Curiously, God's insights never told me whether Bathsheba simply surrendered to the powerful status or will of the King, or the overpowering lust that lay within her own heart as well. Was she a confederate of the King; or was she the victim of a rapacious King *and* a loyal soldier oblivious to the husbandly duties of a man? Would she not have known, either way, of the stoning death that would have faced her for her sin, unless the King simply overpowered her physically? Surely, it would not have been sufficient for her to find "innocence" in having had to submit to the "will" of the King of Israel—a man whom, she would have known, God anointed to do good, not evil!

David Sees Bath-Sheba Bathing, J. James Tissot

3

The Ridding of Uriah

So David sent word to Joab, "Send me Uriah the Hittite." And Joab sent Uriah to David. When Uriah came to him, David asked how Joab and the people fared, and how the war was going. Then David said to Uriah, "Go down to your house, and wash your feet." Uriah went out of the king's house, and there followed him a present from the king. But Uriah slept at the entrance of the king's house with all the servants of his lord, and did not go down to his house. When they told David, "Uriah did not go down to his house," David said to Uriah, "You have just come from a journey. Why did you not go down to your house?" Uriah said to David, "The ark and Israel and Judah remain in booths; and my lord Joab and the servants of my lord are camping in the open field; shall I then go to my house, to eat and to drink, and to lie with my wife? As you live, and as your soul lives, I will not do such a thing." Then David said to Uriah, "Remain here today also, and tomorrow I will send you back." So Uriah remained in Jerusalem that day. On the next day, David invited him to eat and drink in his presence and made him drunk; and in the evening he went out to lie on his couch with the servants of his lord, but he did not go down to his house. In the morn-

The Ridding of Uriah

ing David wrote a letter to Joab, and sent it by the hand of Uriah. In the letter he wrote, "Set Uriah in the forefront of the hardest fighting, and then draw back from him, so that he may be struck down and die." As Joab was besieging the city, he assigned Uriah to the place where he knew there were valiant warriors. The men of the city came out and fought with Joab; and some of the servants of David among the people fell. Uriah the Hittite was killed as well.

(2 Samuel 11:6–17)

I knew more of this sordid business that stained the sheets in the King's chamber, as did so many others who spoke not. I knew that Bathsheba had later sent word to the King that she was with child, and that the child was the King's, for her husband had not been with her. David was not a man who lacked guile. When Uriah returned from battle, he demanded that Uriah go back to his wife, hoping Uriah would be persuaded, when Bathsheba swelled up, that the baby inside her was his. Ever the strategist! And in his strategy to deny his fatherhood of the baby, he was instantly willing to "deny" the baby already alive in its mother's womb. The King of Israel was satisfied to protect himself— from God?—that a child that would come from

"By nature he was not disposed to commit such evil-doing as his relation to Bathsheba involved. God Himself brought him to his crime, that He might say to other sinners: 'Go to David and learn how to repent.'"
(Abodah Zarah 4b–5a)

"Nor, indeed, may David be charged with...adultery. There were extenuating circumstances. In those days it was customary for warriors to give their wives bills of divorce, which were to have validity only if the soldier husbands did not return at the end of the campaign. Uriah having fallen in battle, Bathsheba was a regularly divorced woman."
(Shabbat 56a; Ketubot 9b; Kiddushin 43a; Legends of the Jews, IV)

his own loins would not be the son of the King at all. The King of Israel was boldly willing to deny his son to protect himself!

However one might wish to defend the King's act of lust—that Uriah, as a soldier, at war, had given his wife a conditional bill of divorce lest he be lost in battle (but not found dead) leaving her unable to remarry—his was the carnal sin of adultery entitled to no defense. And his efforts to disguise his conduct were the greatest proof of that fact undeniable!

How could the King not see that a man is married to his wife until the end of time, and beyond? The words of the *k'tubah* are not a contract between a man and a woman, but a covenantal testament between the man, the woman, and God Almighty. The marriage contract was with God!

David's secret was afoot in murmurs. I needed no "vision" to know that the loyal soldier, ignorant of the King's artifice, refused his sire's demand—telling him that he could not honorably stay behind in the arms of Bathsheba whilst the Ark and Joab and his soldiers were encamped on the battlefield's front lines. And David needed no vision from the Lord to realize that only the act of the trained killer, which the King surely was, could "undo" what he had done in the lustful, midnight hour of nights gone by.

But trained killers, cold-blooded strategists, can also prove sinister. David so proved. When Uriah defied the King's command to remain at home, back from battle, beside Bathsheba, David found himself justified in placing in Uriah's hand his own death warrant. Perhaps, in jealousy that Uriah was now the valiant warrior that David no longer was, he told Uriah to bring the General Joab a sealed letter. In it, he told Joab to send Uriah to the forefront of the hottest battle and to counsel his soldiers to withdraw from Uriah *"so that he may be struck down and die."* Indeed, the husband was the "last to know" of his wife's betrayal through intimacy with the King, and, in loyalty to "duty," would never live to learn how the King savagely chose to hide it. Perhaps the King, in envy, wanted to show all of Israel that Uriah, standing at the frontlines alone, was not the warrior David had been when he himself stood *alone* as a child against Goliath.

How I wish I would have had a vision from God *before* Uriah left the palace gates of what David planned for Bathsheba's cuckold. If I had had that vision, I would have had the power to change the future—and I would have done so. For I saw the King's act as nothing less than the act of a murderer disguised in the armor of the King of Israel! And it was murder. Forget the contention that Uriah defied the King's order that he return to his wife, entitling the King to punish his insubordination by taking his life: taking a soldier's life who insisted on fighting, at risk of death, the King's holy war against the enemy. I would have wanted to stop the King

"Moreover, from the first, Bathsheba had been destined by God for David, but by way of punishment for having lightly promised Uriah the Hittite an Israelitish woman to wife, in return for his aid in unfastening the armor of the prostrate Goliath, the king had to undergo bitter trials before he won her." (Unknown Midrash in Al-Sheikh, 2 Sam. 12)

"As for the death of [Bathsheba's] husband, it cannot be laid entirely at David's door, for Uriah had incurred the death penalty by his refusal to take his ease in his own house, according to the king's bidding." (Shabbat 56a; Ketubot 9b; Kiddushin 43a; Legends of the Jews, IV)

no matter his anointment, lest all the House of Israel believe it could defy the Law of God so boldly!

My power as a prophet was, thus, in the end, useless. But not so the powers of David. He didn't need to predict the future, for he exercised the power to cause it. And he did. Uriah was wantonly killed by the friendly fire of his own commander—the King. On that horrible day in the history of our people I was a "blind prophet," as, it seems, God wanted me to be. I would have wanted the assignment to counsel the King on account of his conduct, but my assignment instead was to deliver God's edict. There is no choosing assignments when it comes to being "called" by God!

I learned in due course of Uriah's untimely death, as speculation grew around the kingdom how it happened that he was left alone in battle on the frontlines. When, with a wink, Joab sent David, through a messenger, word of Uriah's death, the King replied, disturbingly, that the General should not be saddened, *"for the sword devours now one and now another."*[1]

When Bathsheba learned of Uriah's death, she mourned his loss. One wonders whether the King even bothered to send her words of his condolence. Surely he did not tell her his murderous role in her husband's death.

But soon enough, when her days of mourning had passed, the King sent for her and they were wed. The baby was born— but none spoke aloud of who its father was, and when he was conceived. Still, without a word uttered by anyone, the Lord surely knew; and He was displeased with what David had done.

---

1. 2 Samuel 11:25.

Death of Uriah, Paul Hardy

4

Nathan Summoned by God

When the mourning was over, David sent and brought her to his house, and she became his wife, and bore him a son. But the thing that David had done displeased the LORD. (2 Samuel 11:27)

"The death of David did not mean the end of his glory and grandeur. It merely caused a change of scene. In the heavenly realm as on earth David ranks among the first. The crown upon his head outshines all others, and whenever he moves out of Paradise to present himself before God, suns, stars, angels, seraphim, and other holy beings run to meet him." (BHM V, 167–68, and VI, 25–26; Sanhedrin 38b; Legends of the Jews, IV)

"...[A]nd the LORD sent Nathan to David. He came to him, and said to him, "There were two men in a certain city, the one rich and the other poor...."

(2 Samuel 12:1)

The speaking task became mine; though I could not alter the future, I alone was called upon to speak it. The word "orphan" describes the child without parent, "widow" and "widower" exist for the spouse who is left behind. But there is no word for the parent who has lost a child—for what word could meaningfully identify such a state of despair? God instructed me to tell the King of Israel what would be in store for him for his sin. And so I was called upon to exercise His will: the "sublime" duty of a prophet of God!

18

I awoke that day from my troubling dream-vision trembling, sweat encompassing my body. I had been told by God to confront the King, a warrior of God, whom the people loved—a man in so many ways their "savior." A killer of those who challenged Israel. The forebear of the Messiah, with all His attributes. A man who seemed, at times, to the Children of Israel, to be what God would appear to be if He chose to be man. And maybe this perception of the Children of Israel led the King to believe that he was, indeed, God on earth, and could do whatever he wanted. What a dangerous road to travel—as if David was destined to become the Son of God!

How, after all, could he otherwise have uttered words, as he once did, so astonishing for any man—saintly or sinner: *"For I have kept the ways of the Lord, and have not wickedly departed from my God. For all his ordinances were before me, and from his statutes I did not turn aside. I was blameless before him, and I kept myself from guilt. Therefore the Lord has recompensed me according to my righteousness, according to my cleanness in his sight."*[1] David, the Anointed, is praised for these words that will live forever as proof of his greatness as God's chosen warrior. But for that anointment and his Godly nature would it not have been sinful for one to proclaim his own rectitude, as he did—even if merited?

"I will give you rest from all your enemies. Moreover the LORD declares to you that the LORD will make you a house. When your days are fulfilled and you lie down with your ancestors, I will raise up your offspring after you, who shall come forth from your body, and I will establish his kingdom. He shall build a house for my name, and I will establish the throne of his kingdom forever."
(2 Samuel 7:11–13)

---

1. 2 Samuel 22:22–25.

19

And I am the man, a man without the anointment of David, who had come to the Palace of that Godly figure once before to deny him the one thing he seemed so urgently to desire—to build the Temple. That day was the only time before when I had the same look on my face as I did when I entered the Palace one week ago. And when I entered the Palace to confront him over Bathsheba and Uriah, the King surely saw it. For reasons I will never understand, though God could have spoken to David, "the Prophet," directly, I instead was called upon to bring that bad news, too, to him. While years ago God told Moses directly how his life would end on the far side of the Jordan, on the day a week ago that I approached David I somehow felt burdened by the belief that if I had been alive on that most sad day for Moses, it somehow would also have been *my* lot to impart the awful news to His servant who spoke to God as no other.

But last week would be different from my earlier approach to David. The day I told him that he would not build the Temple, that his son would do so after David would lie with his forefathers, he recognized that I was delivering the Word of God—that his warrior life that left his hands bloodstained was unsuitable for the architect of God's House. While the message I delivered that day would be painful to him, the "messenger" would surely not be in jeopardy from the King's disillusion.

When I confronted the King with purloining Bathsheba's affection, however, my message would be different—and the King would come to know it the moment our eyes would meet. Prophets of God don't approach kings, or even mortal men, bearing tidings of good fortune. And when these prophets arrive delivering a message of pain to men who present a posture of iron will, they risk, at that very moment, the recipient's belief that the tidings brought are not the message of God at all, but those of the messenger. I feared that, and for myself, greatly—though I, in my rebuking stance, would never show it.

How might I tell the King that his world, as he knew it, would be shattered when I left the Palace, and that he could not change that fate with all the artistry he could summon in a psalm to God.

God came to me with the bad tidings, but not the insight on how to convey them. And even if the King chose not to lop off my head and end my life that day, as he did Goliath's many years before, what would the King say to me (a mere mortal who could not establish that what I had heard in the alleyways beside the Palace about his sinfulness regarding Bathsheba and her murdered husband was true)?

What if the King were to simply say to me "you're a liar" who slanders the Anointed King of Israel and the woman he has taken as a wife—"the mother of the future King of Israel"? What, then, would the life of the "Prophet" Nathan be worth? And even if the King would not "kill" me, as he did Uriah, would he commit me to a life in prison as will occur one day to the Prophet Jeremiah when he brings bad tidings to King Zedekiah of Judah?

"Just as Moses was 'the elect' among the prophets, so was David 'the elect' among the kings." (Tehillim 1, 3)

"David knows how to tend sheep, therefore he shall be the shepherd of my flock Israel." (Tehillim 78, 357)

"When the Philistine drew nearer to meet David, David ran quickly toward the battle line to meet the Philistine [Goliath]. David put his hand in his bag, took out a stone, slung it, and struck the Philistine on his forehead; the stone sank into his forehead, and he fell face down on the ground." (1 Samuel 17:48–49)

21

"At that time the army of the king of Babylon was besieging Jerusalem, and the prophet Jeremiah was confined in the court of the guard that was in the palace of the king of Judah, where King Zedekiah of Judah had confined him. Zedekiah had said, 'Why do you prophesy and say: Thus says the LORD: I am going to give this city into the hand of the king of Babylon, and he shall take it…?'"
(Jeremiah 32:2–3)

As I wiped the sweat that engulfed me having considered these fates, I stared at a looking glass beside my bed and saw nothing but a coward staring back. I spoke to my reflection, the coward, and to myself, saying of the cowardice I saw there: "*You* are that man." And, instantly, I knew what I must do!

5

The Parable

Knowing what one must one do is not the same as knowing how precisely to do it.

How does one confront a man, a man so arrogant as to have *killed* a man, a loyal soldier in the King's army, simply to take his wife—and also a man who truly saw himself, in Samuel's phrase, as "a man after God's own heart"? And in this moment in strategizing how to proceed in facing David, whom I too saw as God's choice to forebear the Messiah, I knew that if I failed in gaining David's contrition he might surrender that exquisite place in God's Design.

If I were to accuse the King, alleging from my own lips his colossal sinfulness, he might simply take my words as meaningless banter of a lesser man, a mortal obliged to bow to the imperial King anointed by God Himself. Or he might reject my words in rash denial. He might remain impervious to his horrible acts.

He might seek to justify them, if perhaps only to himself, as actions compelled by a lowly soldier who refused to comply with a direct order of the Sovereign. Or he would satisfy himself that Uriah richly deserved death, having exhibited the temerity to refer to Joab, the General, as "my Lord" in the presence of a king who alone was Uriah's own earthly lord. He might propose, either in his own mind or in discourse with me (or his counsellors summoned to the encounter), to advocate his own innocence, arguing that the Nation's very security itself was at stake: that it was necessary to kill the defiant soldier, lest his comrades come to believe that they too might defy the King.

He might contend that what he had done was simply warranted as Uriah had extorted from David the "gift" of a beautiful Hebrew woman—gaining that "right" *only* by aiding David when the young warrior, years earlier, could not remove the dead Goliath's helmet after David felled him.

And if all else failed, the King might simply maintain, as may have indeed been true albeit nonjustifying, that Bathsheba was David's *bahsherte*, the woman mystically chosen for him by God Himself at the beginning of time—needing to kill Uriah to fulfill God's Plan that Bathsheba's son would build the Temple!

Still, how does one best bring another man to condemn himself, for self-condemnation was essential? If the King would actually come to blame himself, perhaps not fully knowing what he would be doing at the time, he would likely be unable to retrace his steps.

If, however, he withheld from self-accusation, he might reverse his unwitting act of self-blame and risk losing God's Plan for him.

The idea, still inchoate, began to take shape. If David, through a parable, were brought to examine himself in his own "looking glass," he might be compelled to see his own acts for what they were. In condemning a sinful "wrongdoer" presented to him—a man whom he had no instinct to defend—he might unwittingly condemn himself. And in that act he might begin, in some mystical way, to gain absolution for his reckless descent to the cellar of sin. The parable would make the accusation inescapable to the accused. And so it was born—not in poetry, but rather efficacy.

But I am a lowly prophet, not a strategist. From where did this artifice derive? Had my father or mother, had my grandparents in their absence, used it when *I* was a rebellious young child living in their home? Did the Prophet Samuel, whom I lived alongside during part of his life, use the parable to secure repentance from the House of Israel? Did God come to me in dreams to persuade me that I myself had sinned? Or did it spring elsewhere?

No. I managed to realize, as I prepared to leave for the Palace, from whence indeed it had come: the time of Judges. After the heralded Gideon, the Judge, died, Abimelech killed his father Jerubbaal's seventy sons, which caused the men of Shechem to proclaim him king. Jotham, the lone son of Jerubbaal who survived the slaughter, climbed to the top of Mount Gerizim. He spoke of an orchard of trees that first sought an olive tree, then a fig tree, and then a vine to reign over them. And when they failed to gain a sire over them, they asked a bramble to rule, but it said to them in response: *"If in good faith you are anointing me king over you, then come and take refuge in my shade; but if not, let fire come out of the bramble and devour the cedars of Lebanon."*[1] Three years later, the men of Shechem realized precisely what evil they had wrought in choosing a king for themselves: they rebelled and Abimelech was mortally killed in battle against them.

---

1. Judges 9:15.

The men of Shechem ignored the true meaning of that parable—they failed to see that Jotham spoke about *them*—and needed to endure a murderous king for three more years for not having realized that the parable had nothing to do with trees at all. I prayed with all my heart, as I washed my face with a warm cloth still stalling from my appointed duty, that David would see the words I would say to him for what they truly were meant to say. And I shuddered as I prepared to encounter the King, seeing that the Prophet Samuel showed great earthly wisdom having beseeched God to deny the people a king on earth, for human kings would display the arrogance I needed to address that day.

And in a way in my curious optimism, I prayed for far more. I prayed that the parable would have more significance in the future life of the House of Israel. I longed for it to be a precedent—one that would inspire the King of Israel to repent—to better teach the House of Israel righteousness. For after all, my life was dedicated only to guiding a king, not a people.

Maybe as my blood rushed in my own arrogance I wanted, in my innermost thoughts, to believe that great prophets of the future would also use the device. I saw somehow a future in which, when God's House might somehow lapse into disorder, a rebuking prophet would speak to the renegade Israel of a man, a "beloved," who prized his vineyard more than anything. Although he took every measure possible to produce superior grapes, he destroyed and made them a wasteland when the grapes picked were all sour.[2] And I prayed that the Children of

2. Isaiah 5:1–7.

Israel, if that day should ever come, would see the grapes for what—or *who*—they were.

And perhaps, finally, an almost sinful enthusiasm to answer my call to duty would lead me to reach for even more. I knew that, if I would wisely use my calling, the blood of him whom I would confront before sunset that day, David, would someday flow within the body of the Messiah Himself. How wondrous if the Messiah, when His day will arrive, would also use the parable to guide the House of Israel. That someday, describing a "good neighbor" or some such person,[3] He will inspire Divinely: He will remind the Children of Israel that their eagerness to perform ritual might cause them to sinfully "cross to the other side of the road" to evade their ultimate duty to help one's fellow man.

But my idle daydreams aside, there was and would be no romance, nor glamour, nor kingdom for me in my life and the task that awaited me. Simply God's demand should and would be enough. No Book of Nathan would be needed to tell what my life's mission was to be. All my life's work would be here, right now. People cannot plan glorious lives, but simply must follow God's demands.

Still having gathered myself, I lumbered slowly to the Palace gates, procrastinating in my cowardly state from my commitment to God's command. Somehow it seemed that I arrived too soon, But I was there! There was no turning back.

---

3. Luke 10:26–37.

6

Nathan Confronts David

And the LORD sent Nathan to David. He came to him, and said to him, "There were two men in a certain city, the one rich and the other poor. The rich man had very many flocks and herds; but the poor man had nothing but one little ewe lamb, which he had bought. He brought it up, and it grew up with him and with his children; it used to eat of his meager fare, and drink from his cup, and lie in his bosom, and it was like a daughter to him. Now there came a traveler to the rich man, and he was loath to take one of his own flock or herd to prepare for the wayfarer who had come to him, but he took the poor man's lamb, and prepared that for the guest who had come to him." Then David's anger was greatly kindled against the man. He said to Nathan, "As the LORD lives, the man who has done this deserves to die; he shall restore the lamb fourfold, because he did this thing, and because he had no pity." Nathan said to David, "You are the man! Thus says the LORD, the God of Israel: I anointed you king over Israel, and I rescued you from the hand of Saul; I gave you your master's house, and your master's wives into your bosom, and gave you the house of Israel and of Judah; and if that had been too little, I would have added as much more. Why have you

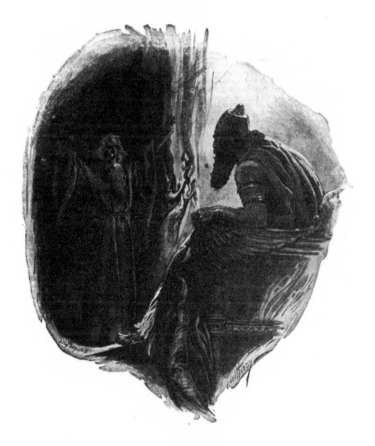

Thou Art the Man, Paul Hardy

despised the word of the LORD, *to do what is evil in his sight? You have struck down Uriah the Hittite with the sword, and have taken his wife to be your wife, and have killed him with the sword of the Ammonites. Now therefore the sword shall never depart from your house, for you have despised me, and have taken the wife of Uriah the Hittite to be your wife. Thus says the* LORD: *I will raise up trouble against you from within your own house; and I will take your wives before your eyes, and give them to your neighbor, and he shall lie with your wives in the sight of this very sun. For you did it secretly; but I will do this thing before all Israel, and before the sun." David said to Nathan, "I have sinned against the* LORD." *Nathan said to David, "Now the* LORD *has put away your sin; you shall not die."* (2 Samuel 12:1–13)

The King greeted me and, seeing the cold look on my face, bid his advisors and servants to depart from our midst. I saw it incumbent on me to be unvacillating in my approach to the King. Neither he nor I engaged in trivial greetings and gestures of civility. No mention of family or affairs of state or even a brief *"dvar Torah"* (a reflection on a subject of God's Law, appropriate for a visit from one "Man of God" to another). He knew!

At first, I wanted to ask him of the health of Bathsheba and his newborn baby, who remarkably seems without a name. Who would not so inquire, except a Prophet of God about to remonstrate the King over his adultery with that woman who bore him the son? But I suppressed my inquiry.

Instead, I immediately pressed forward: *"There were two men in a certain city, the one rich and the other poor. The rich*

30

man had very many flocks and herds; but the poor man had
nothing but one little ewe lamb, which he had bought. He
brought it up, and it grew up with him and with his children; it
used to eat of his meager fare, and drink from his cup, and lie
in his bosom, and it was like a daughter to him."[1] The King
seemed angered that I wasted his time with seeming triviality.

Yet, I continued to bore on: *"Now there came a traveler to
the rich man, and he was loath to take one of his own flock or
herd to prepare for the wayfarer who had come to him, but he
took the poor man's lamb, and prepared that for the guest who
had come to him."*[2] Still recklessly oblivious to what I was saying to him, and about him, the King's anger now turned to the
rich man in the parable: He said: *"As the LORD lives, the man
who has done this deserves to die; he shall restore the lamb fourfold, because he did this thing, and because he had no pity."*[3]
The King had already pronounced his own death sentence, but
didn't realize it.

I was astonished, and afraid. The King was already in a murderous rage—he demanded "death" for a foolish rich man who
fed a traveler using a sheep of a poor man, over his own. What
would he demand to avenge the reckless words of a minor
"prophet" who would boldly slander the King and his wife,
when he, the Anointed King, clearly did not see the image in
the looking glass pointing back at him? I had no place to turn
having gone down this road—for if I chose, now, to stop short
of causing his self-condemnation with his own words, my head

---

1. 2 Samuel 12:1–3.
2. 2 Samuel 12:4.
3. 2 Samuel 12:5–6.

might soon lie on the Palace's floor beside my body: the King did not see himself as the parable's "the rich man." It seemed as if time stood still during our momentary encounter as the King's face reddened with each moment. He waited impatiently to hear my next words that would presumably decipher the uncharted words I had so far spoken.

And, again, perhaps due to the cowardice I saw in my looking glass that morning, my parable never spoke of the worst of the King's conduct. I alluded to his "taking" of a ewe of the poor man, but never the "murder" of the poor man. Those who reflect on this tragic episode in the life of David should not withdraw from recognizing the array of his sinful conduct for what it was.

"You Are That Man"

I could hesitate no longer: *"You are that man"*—the very words I told myself earlier this day. The look in the King's eyes yielded meager hint at recognition.

Still, I didn't have the inner strength to simply tell him what God had in store for him. Having said *"you are that man,"* I timidly now said, *"Thus, says the LORD, the God of Israel,"* not wanting him to think, for a moment longer, that what would come from my lips was my decree, not God's: *"I anointed you king over Israel, and I rescued you from the hand of Saul; I gave you your master's house, and your master's wives into your bosom, and gave you the house of Israel and of Judah; and if that had been too little, I would have added as much more. Why have you despised the word of the LORD, to do what is evil in his sight? You have struck down Uriah the Hittite with the sword, and have taken his wife to be your wife, and have killed him with the sword of the Ammonites.*"[4]

The King no longer looked in my direction. He now understood the parable. No longer did I fear that he would believe that this audacious little Prophet, not God, was his accuser. Still, I wondered why he needed me to level the accusation. Did he not know how flagrantly he was transgressing God's Law as his sinfulness occurred?

The King now fell into his throne. I began to pity him despite all he had done that brought me to the Palace steps. For a moment I almost tried to "visit" God to ask that I might enjoin that which would still come from my lips—but a cowardice of another sort took hold. Was it "cowardice" or blind obedience to His Will? And, in truth, I still could not fathom, though the King was already seeming to fall apart, what would come from my lips, nor what the King would say—and whether, indeed, his still reddening face would manifest itself in words, or the drawing of his terribly swift sword.

Words continued to come from my lips, almost uncontrollably: "*Now therefore the sword shall never depart from your house, for you have despised me, and have taken the wife of Uriah the Hittite to be your wife.*"[5] For the moment he seemed to recover. His red face glared at me as a stone. I continued, invoking the Word of God: "*I will raise up trouble against you from within your own house; and I will take your wives before your eyes, and give them to your neighbor, and he shall lie with your wives in the sight of this very sun. For you did it secretly;*

---

4. 2 Samuel 12:7–9.
5. 2 Samuel 12:10.

"The LORD is my shepherd,
I shall not want.
He makes me lie down in
green pastures;
he leads me beside still waters;
he restores my soul.
He leads me in right paths
for his name's sake.

Even though I walk through the
darkest valley, I fear no evil;
for you are with me;
your rod and your staff—
they comfort me.

You prepare a table before me
in the presence of my enemies;
you anoint my head with oil;
my cup overflows.

Surely goodness and mercy
shall follow me
all the days of my life,
and I shall dwell in the house of
the LORD my whole life long."
(Psalm 23)

but I will do this thing before all Israel, and before the sun"[6] I had just told the Anointed King of Israel that the sword would never leave his house, and he surely understood that he, the King, would not be holding that sword. And beyond that, he had taken a man's wife; and, thus, his wives, in punishment, beyond the death of his child, would be taken from him by his own son—a poetic "eye for an eye."

Decades, it seemed, passed during which the King's silence deafened me. Perhaps, while I still stood before him, the great psalmist would compose those lofty words for which he was so much heralded. Or perhaps he would continue to say nothing. Perhaps, he would simply dispense with me and ask to be left to his thoughts or other duties of state—all the while maintaining a bold exterior. But, in an instant, the words came quickly without embellishment: *"Chatassi L'Adonai"*—*"I have sinned against the LORD."*[7] There was nothing else to say. Nothing else worth saying! And to reveal, at that moment, my own sadness in having told David his punishment would detract from my duty as God's messenger.

---

6. 2 Samuel 12:11–12.
7. 2 Samuel 12:13.

Nathan Confronts David

I could not have foretold that he would say those words. And I had come to the Palace recognizing the possibility that even if he did not slay me, he would self-justify, or mitigate. But he did neither. And there would be "some" good report in what I would say to him—tidings not *instantly* available for any other man who sinned against God, as did David. For waiting but a moment, I told him: *"Now the LORD has put away your sin; you shall not die."*[8]

He showed no relief—he too was Prophet and probably now, if not before, realized there was more to come. And there surely was! In looking back, though, I now see also that the expression on his face at that instant was a look of disbelief—the look of a man who could not rely on what I had said. The look of a man who believed I might say one thing in one instant, and then reverse my words.

In looking at it, I acted with almost sinister affect in how I presented this news to him. For as the King's color somewhat returned to his face, having heard that his life had been spared, I again could not hold back my words: *"Nevertheless, because by this deed you have utterly scorned the LORD, the child that is born to you shall die."*[9] Why would I tell him of his baby's impending death *after* I told him that his own life would be

"In a measure David was indebted for his life to Adam. At first only three hours of existence had been allotted to him. When God caused all future generations to pass in review before Adam, he besought God to give David seventy of the thousand years destined for him. A deed of gift, signed by God and the angel Metatron, was drawn up. Seventy years were legally conveyed from Adam to David, and in accordance with Adam's wishes, beauty, dominion, and poetical gift went with them." (PRE 19; BAR 14.12; Legends of the Jews, IV)

---

8. 2 Samuel 12:13.
9. 2 Samuel 12:14.

35

spared? Would it have been worse for the King to tell him that the baby would die, but he would live? Or did I deliver the news in that order because I simply decided to tell it to the King in the order of how I perceived its importance to him—his own life over the baby's?

And perhaps, not needing to deal with the affairs of state and how the world must follow the providence of the history God dictates, I was too human or sensitive to the simple issue before me that day. David, though, concentrated on his linkage to Adam, the First of Men. He knew that Adam, from near the beginning of time, had persuaded God to extend David's life beyond the few hours that he was initially to live, to fulfill his mission to God—no matter who might fall along the roadside. For a man the likes of David, even in a moment of torment, it was more important, despite all, that he live on; and he was relieved by that reality, even if an innocent baby would be the sacrifice burnt on the altar for his sin. For a conqueror like David, born to shield the Children of Israel from their enemies, born to lead them in battle, and born to spawn the Messiah who would lead them until the end of time, the prophecy needed fulfillment. It needed the continuity of his very life to make it so. Duty sometimes makes men cold-blooded (even in dealing with their own children)!

Nathan Reproving David for his Crime, Richard Westall

7

"The Sword Shall Never Depart from Your House"

*"Why have you despised the word of the L*ORD*, to do what is evil in his sight? You have struck down Uriah the Hittite with the sword, and have taken his wife to be your wife, and have killed him with the sword of the Ammonites. Now therefore the sword shall never depart from your house, for you have despised me, and have taken the wife of Uriah the Hittite to be your wife. Thus says the L*ORD*: I will raise up trouble against you from within your own house; and I will take your wives before your eyes, and give them to your neighbor, and he shall lie with your wives in the sight of this very sun. For you did it secretly; but I will do this thing before all Israel, and before the sun." David said to Nathan, "I have sinned against the L*ORD*." Nathan said to David, "Now the L*ORD* has put away your sin; you shall not die. Nevertheless, because by this deed you have utterly scorned the L*ORD*, the child that is born to you shall die." Then Nathan went to his house. The L*ORD* struck the child that Uriah's wife bore to David, and it became very ill.* (2 Samuel 12:9–15)

On the seventh day the child died. And the servants of David were afraid to tell him that the child was dead; for they said, "While the child was still alive, we spoke to him, and he did not listen to us; how then can we tell him the child is dead? He may do himself some harm."

(2 Samuel 12:18)

Some time passed. David's son Absalom had a beautiful sister whose name was Tamar; and David's son Amnon fell in love with her. Amnon was so tormented that he made himself ill because of his sister Tamar, for she was a virgin and it seemed impossible to Amnon to do anything to her....Amnon said to [Jonadab], "I love Tamar, my brother Absalom's sister." Jonadab said to him, "Lie down on your bed, and pretend to be ill; and when your father comes to see you, say to him, 'Let my sister Tamar come and give me something to eat, and prepare the food in my sight, so that I may see it and eat it from her hand.'" So Amnon lay down, and pretended to be ill; and when the king came to see him, Amnon said to the king, "Please let my sister Tamar come and make a couple of cakes in my sight, so that I may eat from her hand."

Then David sent home to Tamar, saying, "Go to your brother Amnon's house, and prepare food for him."...Then she took the pan and set [cakes] out before him, but he refused to eat. Amnon said, "Send out everyone from me." So everyone went out from him. Then Amnon said to Tamar, "Bring the food into the

39

chamber, so that I may eat from your hand." So Tamar took the cakes she had made, and brought them into the chamber to Amnon her brother. But when she brought them near him to eat, he took hold of her, and said to her, "Come, lie with me, my sister." She answered him, "No, my brother, do not force me; for such a thing is not done in Israel; do not do anything so vile! As for me, where could I carry my shame?...Now therefore, I beg you, speak to the king; for he will not withhold me from you." But he would not listen to her; and being stronger than she, he forced her and lay with her.

(2 Samuel 13:1–14)

Then Absalom commanded his servants, "Watch when Amnon's heart is merry with wine, and when I say to you, 'Strike Amnon,' then kill him. Do not be afraid; have I not myself commanded you? Be courageous and valiant." So the servants of Absalom did to Amnon as Absalom had commanded. (2 Samuel 13:28–29)

Absalom used to rise early and stand beside the road into the gate; and when anyone brought a suit before the king for judgment, Absalom would call out and say, "From what city are you?" When the person said, "Your servant is of such and such a tribe in Israel," Absalom would say, "See, your claims are good and right; but there is no one deputed by the king to hear you." Absalom said moreover, "If only I were judge in the

land! Then all who had a suit or cause might come to me, and I would give them justice." Whenever people came near to do obeisance to him, he would put out his hand and take hold of them, and kiss them. Thus Absalom did to every Israelite who came to the king for judgment; so Absalom stole the hearts of the people of Israel. (2 Samuel 15:2–6)

While Absalom was offering the sacrifices, he sent for Ahithophel the Gilonite, David's counselor, from his city Giloh. The conspiracy grew in strength, and the people with Absalom kept increasing. A messenger came to David, saying, "The hearts of the Israelites have gone after Absalom." (2 Samuel 15:12–13)

Absalom happened to meet the servants of David. Absalom was riding on his mule, and the mule went under the thick branches of a great oak. His head caught fast in the oak, and he was left hanging between heaven and earth, while the mule that was under him went on. (2 Samuel 18:9)

The king said to the Cushite, "Is it well with the young man Absalom?" The Cushite answered, "May the enemies of my lord the king, and all who rise up to do you harm, be like that young man." The king was deeply moved, and went up to the chamber over the gate, and wept; and as he went, he said, "O my son Absalom, my son, my son Absalom! Would I had died instead of you, O Absalom, my son, my son!" (2 Samuel 18:32–33)

41

Then Adonijah son of Haggith came to Bathsheba, Solomon's mother. She asked, "Do you come peaceably?" He said, "Peaceably." Then he said, "May I have a word with you?" She said, "Go on." He said, "You know that the kingdom was mine, and that all Israel expected me to reign; however, the kingdom has turned about and become my brother's, for it was his from the Lord. And now I have one request to make of you; do not refuse me." She said to him, "Go on." He said, "Please ask King Solomon—he will not refuse you—to give me Abishag the Shunammite as my wife." Bathsheba said, "Very well; I will speak to the king on your behalf." So Bathsheba went to King Solomon, to speak to him on behalf of Adonijah. The king rose to meet her, and bowed down to her; then he sat on his throne, and had a throne brought for the king's mother, and she sat on his right. Then she said, "I have one small request to make of you; do not refuse me." And the king said to her, "Make your request, my mother; for I will not refuse you." She said, "Let Abishag the Shunammite be given to your brother Adonijah as his wife." King Solomon answered his mother, "And why do you ask Abishag the Shunammite for Adonijah? Ask for him the kingdom as well! For he is my elder brother; ask not only for him but also for the priest Abiathar and for Joab son of Zeruiah!" Then King Solomon swore by the LORD, "So may God do to me, and more also, for Adonijah has devised this scheme at the risk of his life! Now therefore as the LORD lives, who has

> *established me and placed me on the throne of my father*
> *David, and who has made me a house as he promised,*
> *today Adonijah shall be put to death." So King Solomon*
> *sent Benaiah son of Jehoiada; he struck him down, and*
> *he died.*   (1 Kings 2:13–25)

What I withheld from the King that day did not have the immediacy of the baby's death or the direct linkage to Bathsheba. But it would have shown him that his sinfulness would, indeed, not be commuted soon or simply by the death of the infant. The torment of his life for his sins would never leave him, even in death.

Years before the incident of Bathsheba, David, entitled by right to a polygamous state, had married Ahinoam the Jezreelitess who gave birth to his firstborn Ammon. And his wife Abigail gave birth to a second son Chileab. Later, in battle, the King took Maacah, daughter of Talmar, king of Geshur. She was an *eishat yi'fat toar,* a beautiful woman—the captive right of a warrior in combat. She would later give birth to his son Absalom and his daughter Tamar.

But years from now Ammon, unbeknownst to the King, will become lovesick for his beautiful, virgin, half sister Tamar, full sister of Absalom. Distraught by his love for her, he will feign sickness to lure her to his bedchamber to *"eat food from your hand."* When she refuses his wish to have her, he will take her by force. The rape of the daughter of David by his own son will be a further stain on the House of David; but David himself, though hearing of the deed, will do nothing. Absalom will avenge his sister's disgrace by himself killing his own brother.

Tamar, J. James Tissot

The bloodshed will not end there. The beautiful Absalom, having avenged his sister's rape, will not be satisfied to be a mere Prince of Israel. He will take the concubines of his father, the King; and at the same Palace rooftop where his father, the King, took Bathsheba as his own, he will have them for himself—as both an act of lust and mutiny against the King. He will rise up in military rebellion against David to take his throne; and he will die when his long flowing hair will be caught in low-hanging branches while he rides in battle against the King's troops. The mule he will ride will have run out from under him, leaving Absalom hanging by his hair—only to be killed later by ten of David's servants who will avenge his offense against his father. David, the King, will suffer, again, from the loss of a son—even though a son who will be killed, finally, for his insurrection against him.

And there will be yet another instance of fratricide among the sons of David. After her mourning subsides, Bathsheba will give birth to another son, Solomon, whom, at God's direction, I will name "Jedidiah"—"beloved of God." He will later build the Temple. In love for her, David will promise Bathsheba that Solomon (Jedidiah) will rule Israel after he dies. As the King will near death, another son, however, Adonijah, not born to Bathsheba, will claim and take the throne behind the back of the sickly King. Bathsheba and I will come to the King's deathbed as a young maiden warms him, and David will acknowledge to us the promise to the Queen and honor his word.

But although, after David's death, Adonijah will feign to surrender to Solomon's right to the throne, he will ask the King's mother, Bathsheba, to petition Solomon to give him

Death of Absalom, Paul Hardy

Abishag the Shunammite, the beautiful young concubine to the now-deceased King David, who had ministered to him in the waning days of his life. When Solomon will be told by Bathsheba of Adonijah's request, he will know it for what it is—a ruse to reassert his entitlement to the throne of his father. Solomon, a man whose name ironically connotes peace, will have his brother Adonijah killed (although David will not know it in his lifetime).

Three sons of David will die by the sword, a daughter will be raped, and an infant son has died already—all because of the sinfulness of the father. And I knew all of this future the day I came to the Palace, but could do nothing about it! What worth the ability to prophesy? And is it not better that I chose to keep most of my vision to myself?

In truth, I could not bring myself, when I confronted the King that day, a week ago, to tell him what God truly meant when, in the Name of the Lord, I told David: *"I will take your wives before your eyes, and give them to your neighbor, and he shall lie with your wives in the sight of this very sun."*[1] I could not tell him what his sinfulness will have truly wrought. I could not bring myself to tell the King that his daughter would be raped by his eldest son, who would be killed by another, mutinous son, who would die—killed by ten of the King's servants for the ten concubines he stole from his father. I could not tell him that after his death yet another son would be killed by his son, the King, born to build the Temple with hands not stained by the blood that blemished the hands of his father. It would have been too much for any man to bear! I believe—even too

---

1. 2 Samuel 12:11.

47

much to bear for a King, as David, born to fulfill God's destiny no matter what might stand in his way!

Even the words I uttered to him: *"The sword shall never depart from your house,"* seemed too much. But, I thought, perhaps the poet-King might be able to receive them, that day, as mere metaphor.

However he accepted my brief words to him, our conversation was at an end. I had just told a man that his healthy baby would die—*because* of him! I gave no words of condolence, and David sought none from me. He was the King. Kings, warrior kings, even psalmist kings, stand tall in the face of loss, even the loss of life.

I extended my hand to David in peace; his hand was cold and quickly withdrawn from mine. I was the messenger! And if, as some of the King's supplicants believed, David harbored the notion that he himself was destined to be the Messiah, what was his thinking now?

8

A Psalm of Contrition

Have mercy on me, O God,
*   according to your steadfast love;*
according to your abundant mercy
*   blot out my transgressions.*
Wash me thoroughly from my iniquity,
*   and cleanse me from my sin.*

For I know my transgressions,
*   and my sin is ever before me.*
Against you, you alone, have I sinned,
*   and done what is evil in your sight,*
so that you are justified in your sentence
*   and blameless when you pass judgment.*
Indeed, I was born guilty,
*   a sinner when my mother conceived me.*

You desire truth in the inward being;
*   therefore teach me wisdom in my secret heart.*
Purge me with hyssop, and I shall be clean;
*   wash me, and I shall be whiter than snow.*
Let me hear joy and gladness;
*   let the bones that you have crushed rejoice.*

Hide your face from my sins,
and blot out all my iniquities.

Create in me a clean heart, O God,
and put a new and right spirit within me.
Do not cast me away from your presence,
and do not take your holy spirit from me.
Restore to me the joy of your salvation,
and sustain in me a willing spirit.

Then I will teach transgressors your ways,
and sinners will return to you.
Deliver me from bloodshed, O God,
O God of my salvation,
and my tongue will sing aloud
of your deliverance.

O Lord, open my lips,
and my mouth will declare your praise.
For you have no delight in sacrifice;
if I were to give a burnt offering,
you would not be pleased.

Psalm 51

As I reached the foot of the Palace steps, I heard the chanting words of the King who had begun to compose a psalm. The last words that I heard as I departed the Palace were: *"Indeed, I was born guilty, a sinner when my mother conceived me."*[1] I asked

---

1. Psalm 51:5.

50

David's Penance, Byzantine miniature, 10th century,
Paris, Bibliothèque National

myself whether the King did not take too-easy license in suggesting his *mother's* "sin," when his own sin was the only one in issue that day. And given his grave sin over Bathsheba I wonder, even today, about the psalm he composed that I now know in its fullness. Although in it he beseeched God for absolution for his acts—in pious, exquisite words that no other man could emulate—how did he never address his "responsibility" by describing the specificity of his actions: the emblem of *t'shuvah* (repentance)? He spoke of his "transgression," but not what he did.

I realized, too, at that moment, why, whether born in sin or not, I was not born to be a king or great man. In doing so, I wondered how great men who silently yield to the Word of God, as did David in that instant, can do so stoically without questions. How can they not ask questions that humans, like myself, incapable of unyielding obedience to God, may see as God wanting to hear from them?

If I were David that day, would I not have said to God, when hearing that my baby would die for *my* sin: "Take me, not him"? If I were Abraham when he was directed by God to take Isaac to the *Akedah,* would I not have said to God: "Take me, not him"?

Why did David not ask that? And is he to be praised for unyielding obedience to God's Word—as he will be, righteously, for saying those simple words to me: *"I have sinned against God"?* And would it have been disobedient to God for David to have asked of me when I still stood before him seven days ago, whether there was not another way to pay the wages of his sin— to cause the death of the guilty, not the innocent? And maybe for David, at that moment, the answer was just that he simply did not care enough about the baby, only that he was the King, the Anointed King of Israel—and that was what mattered.

When hearing of the death of Absalom who will die in mutiny against him, David will lament, uttering those profound words *"O my son Absalom, my son, my son Absalom! Would I had died instead of you, O Absalom, my son, my son!"*[2] Will he finally come to realize the wages of his sin in a way that he did not a week ago when I came to him? Or, despite all, will it be that he will come to love Absalom as he never loved the baby? Can he love a perfidious son who will defy him, even to the point of a knife, more than the faultless baby born to the true love of his life? Is it that the baby's innocence was beside the point—the King was able to try to "erase" the baby from his lineage while Uriah lived, recognizing that it would have been a constant reminder to everyone of the King's clay feet? And maybe it was that I simply held no credibility for David; that despite my supposed "status" of a prophet of God, he simply did not accept it when I first told him that his baby would die, but was able to see Absalom's cold body before him.

Still and all, the curious look on David's face when I told him that he himself would not die still haunts me. And I fear that the look is a reflection on me, not him. My word was not, to him, reliable—and a prophet who is not dependable in stating the future, when the future can be foretold by the facts within his ken, is only a false prophet. And, I am troubled that when the sleep of exhaustion soon overcomes me, the Lord will come to me again, making the forecast of doom that I gave to David inside the Palace a week ago be worsened. I am concerned

---

2. 2 Samuel 18:33.

that I spoke to David that day of a future that would save him and doom his baby, but that I prophesied to him in error: that the King too would die. For I have given him false prophecy before. Overall, I am, as the day nears its end, fearful that the false word I gave him before may have somehow led him to his fated encounter with Bathsheba.

9

"The Ark of God Stays in a Tent"

David again gathered all the chosen men of Israel, thirty thousand. David and all the people with him set out and went from Baale-judah, to bring up from there the ark of God, which is called by the name of the LORD of hosts who is enthroned on the cherubim. They carried the ark of God on a new cart, and brought it out of the house of Abinadab, which was on the hill. Uzzah and Ahio, the sons of Abinadab, were driving the new cart.... (2 Samuel 6:1–3)

....and when those who bore the ark of the LORD had gone six paces, he sacrificed an ox and a fatling. David danced before the LORD with all his might; David was girded with a linen ephod. So David and all the house of Israel brought up the ark of the LORD with shouting, and with the sound of the trumpet. As the ark of the LORD came into the city of David, Michal daughter of Saul looked out of the window, and saw King David leaping and dancing before the LORD; and she despised him in her heart. They brought in the ark of the LORD, and set it in its place, inside the tent that David had pitched for it; and David offered burnt offerings and offerings of well-being before

55

Michal Despises David, J. James Tissot

the LORD. *When David had finished offering the burnt
offerings and the offerings of well-being, he blessed the
people in the name of the LORD of hosts, and distributed
food among all the people, the whole multitude of Israel,
both men and women, to each a cake of bread, a portion
of meat, and a cake of raisins. Then all the people went
back to their homes. David returned to bless his house-
hold. But Michal the daughter of Saul came out to meet
David, and said, "How the king of Israel honored himself
today, uncovering himself today before the eyes of his servants' maids, as any vulgar fellow might shamelessly
uncover himself!"* (2 Samuel 6:13–20)

How did it occur that I gave David "false" prophecy? In times
past, as warrior King, David, leading sometimes thirty thousand
men in battle, carried forth the Ark of the Covenant in support of
the House of Israel. He protected the Ark and honored God, not
himself, in its carriage. He celebrated the Ark, because of his
Master, so joyously and ardently, that he even incurred the wrath
of his wife, Michal, daughter of Saul (whom he had succeeded),
who failed to recognize the reason for his intense devotion. Seeing
him dancing before the Ark all she could say—indeed, unfairly—
was: *"How the king of Israel honored himself today, uncovering
himself today before the eyes of his servants' maids, as any vulgar
fellow might shamelessly uncover himself!"*[1] God left her barren
until she died for so deriding the King.

Michal had been faithful to David even when her own father,
Saul, in jealousy of David, took her from him and gave her to

---

1. 2 Samuel 6:20.

"When David had finished speaking to Saul, the soul of Jonathan was bound to the soul of David, and Jonathan loved him as his own soul." (1 Samuel 18:1) another man, Palti. In losing her love, then, over the incident of the Ark, David surely concluded that "love" was only tentative. His love of her brother Jonathan, who, too, stood beside David against the vengeful wishes of his own father, had also been cut short by Jonathan's death in battle against the Philistines. Love, for David, however intense, may have been seen as fleeting, and influenced his willingness to seize it—as he did in taking Bathsheba.

His intense devotion to God was different. He seized upon his love for God in celebrating the Ark of the Covenant—but *that* love, which honors David, led him, more than anything, to desire to be the man to build the Temple. So when his battles had subsided and the King dwelt in his Palace, God gave him respite from those around him, from all his enemies.

The King asked that I come to him, and he said to me: *"See now, I am living in a house of cedar, but the ark of God stays in a tent."*[2] They were simple words, but the King's face said that he loved God in a way that even his wife, daughter of Saul, could not comprehend—that his love for her was now over. Struck by David's devotion to God and negation of himself despite all that *Dovid Hamelech,* David the King, had done for Israel as a militarist and king, my words came effortlessly: *"Go, do all that you have in mind; for the Lord is with you."*[3] I wondered later, though, when I heard of his self-indulgence with Bathsheba, whether his overwhelming "devotion" to and "love" for God in wanting to build the Temple was not, in the end, a devotion to self—a "vanity" that would become his undoing.

2. 2 Samuel 7:2.
3. 2 Samuel 7:3.

Still, at that moment, the Divine Spirit had rested upon David, and I presumed that the inspiration to build the Temple was also from God. The Torah had taught me that when God had given the King of Israel respite from his enemies, he was to build the Temple. I never saw on the face of any man the look of joy I saw on David's after I said those words: *"God is with you!"* I reflexively spoke the words that came to my lips.

"Go and tell my servant David: Thus says the LORD: *Are you the one to build me a house to live in?...*

When your days are fulfilled and you lie down with your ancestors, I will raise up your offspring after you, who shall come forth from your body, and I will establish his kingdom. He shall build a house for my name, and I will establish the throne of his kingdom forever."
(2 Samuel 7:5, 12–13)

But God didn't place them there. They were not words of prophecy—but words of aspiration, words of yearning that seemed so right that very moment. In my life I often said "God is with you," to give people comfort to pursue their life's dreams that were good and noble, and within their grasp. Those words, too, were prayers for blessings asking God's intercession, or grace, to make their dreams come true. One need not be a prophet to offer his blessings.

But by midnight after I spoke, thus, to David, I realized I should have been far more careful—that I should have told the King that I was "asking" for a future, not "seeing" it. God came to me that very night to promptly reverse what I had told the King, lest the King, known for his ready commitment to task, immediately begin to build a House of God, when, in truth, he was not "chosen" for it. And now I would have to tell the King of Israel, whose own "house" was now loveless, that he could not refocus his love into building God's.

10

When God Had Come to Nathan

God had come to me that night saying that He had not dwelled in a House from the Exodus to this day; but has gone about in a tent and in a tabernacle. *"Wherever I have moved about among all the people of Israel, did I ever speak a word with any of the tribal leaders of Israel, whom I commanded to shepherd my people Israel, saying, 'Why have you not built me a house of cedar?'"*[1] He told me to tell David that He had been with David always—that He had taken him from the sheepfold to be a ruler over His people and *"have made you a great name."* I would further be instructed to tell David that He had planted His people, and He will give David rest from his enemies and the children of wickedness: *"And God will tell you that a house will God make for you."* Finally, God said that when David is laid to rest *"I will raise up your offspring after you, who shall come forth from your body, and I will establish his kingdom. He shall build a house for my name, and I will establish the throne of his kingdom forever. I will be a father to him, and he shall be a son to me....Your house and your kingdom shall be made sure forever before me; your throne shall be established forever."*[2]

---

1. 2 Samuel 7:7.
2. 2 Samuel 7:12–16.

60

Nathan Reproaches David, J. James Tissot

"When David heard Nathan's message for him, he began to tremble, and he said: 'Ah, verily, God had found me unworthy to erect His sanctuary.' But God replied with these words: 'Nay, the blood shed by thee I consider as sacrificial blood, but I do not care to have thee build the Temple, because then it would be eternal and indestructible.'" (PR 2, 7a–7b; Mekilta Shirah 1, 3–b; Legends of the Jews, IV)

"Joseph also went from the town of Nazareth in Galilee to Judea, to the city of David called Bethlehem, because he was descended from the house and family of David." (Luke 2:4)

I went to the Palace at sunup—not wishing to tarry, as God instructed me. What would the King think of me, and how would he react? Perhaps the knowledge that his throne would be secure forever would be enough to satisfy him—for I would tell him, *in prophecy*, not in mere aspiration as the day before, that "never again" would the enemies of Israel override or seek to defeat the City of David. That was the God-given "prophecy" of a prophet of God— and it will surely come true, will it not? For that is prophecy!

I could not perceive the King's acceptance of my words. He was a poet—poets sometimes camouflage their true feelings in the beauty of their words and rhymes. Over a lifetime he composed sonnets to God that were remarkable. But one can never tell for certain in merely listening to one's words whether they are sincere or contrived.

The King said all that one would have wanted to hear him say though gravely disappointed, as he surely was, in hearing the report. He went before the Ark of the Lord, in my presence. He said: *"For you, O LORD of hosts, the God of Israel, have made this revelation to your servant, saying, 'I will build you a house'; therefore your servant has found courage to pray this prayer to you. And now, O Lord GOD, you are*

62

*God, and your words are true, and you have promised this good
thing to your servant; now therefore may it please you to bless
the house of your servant, so that it may continue forever before
you; for you, O Lord GOD, have spoken, and with your blessing
shall the house of your servant be blessed forever."*[3]

I was pleased, and relieved. It appeared that the King had
not, in the absence of Michal's love, devoted himself to building
a "house" of another sort. The King had now spoken directly to
God, and what I had mistakenly told him yesterday seemed no
longer of moment. His words said he was "satisfied" that the
House would be built by his offspring.

---

3. 2 Samuel 7:27–29.

11

David Seeks God's Test

But I was misinformed; he was not satisfied. Men of steel, indeed, men who are oracles themselves, aren't so easily weaned from their true desires, even when "Men of God" tell them God's Plan. And this man of steel was able to reverse his stated "acceptance" of God's Word that he was not to be God's architect, as quickly as I could tell him one day that God was "with him," but, the very next day, that God was not.

That very night, David beckoned to God from his, then, loveless bedchamber. He had not accepted the "defeat" of his lust to build God's House that he had seemed to be reconciled to in his poetry. And he was still buoyed in confidence to overcome God's Will, by my words that *"God is with you."*

Invoking that very phrase, he complained to God: the people say God of Abraham, God of Isaac, God of Jacob, and why not God of David? God replied that the patriarchs "have been tried by Me, but thou hast not been proved." David said: "Then examine me, O Lord, and try me." And God finally said that He would prove David and even grant him what He did not give the patriarchs. God said that He would tell David beforehand that David would fall into temptation through a woman. It was astonishing to me—David sought a test that Abraham, Isaac, and Jacob would never have the temerity to seek, and although told by God Himself that he would fail it, he could not accept defeat even from God. Vanity!

David, however, smiled to himself, inwardly confident—indeed, "knowing"—that he would survive the test; that his love for God would prevail over any mundane, sensual lust. My words, "God is with you," reinforced his strength of spirit.

And he took those words as "truth"—that my withdrawal from them the day after I uttered them to him was part of his "test." He convinced himself that when he would defeat the temptation of the woman God would place in his way, Israel would come, with God's approval, to call the Lord "God *of David*"—a David then worthy to build God's House. For without needing to even utter a word to himself, he saw the Temple as his destiny, as if to say—"God is with me: the Prophet Nathan, Man of God, has told me so." Prophet Nathan, Man of God, *Seer of All!*

"It came about thus: [David] once complained to God: 'O Lord of the world, why do people say God of Abraham, God of Isaac, God of Jacob, and why not God of David?' The answer came: 'Abraham, Isaac, and Jacob were tried by me, but thou hast not yet been proved.' David entreated: 'Then examine me, O Lord, and try me.' And God said: 'I shall prove thee, and I shall even grant thee what I did not grant the Patriarchs. I shall tell thee beforehand that thou wilt fall into temptation through a woman.'"
(Legends of the Jews, IV, p. 104)

One wonders whether when he stood atop the Palace roof gazing at the siren Bathsheba and summoned her to him, he even realized that *she* was "the test." Or did he simply believe that he was entitled to her, and to kill Uriah, because on the day David slew Goliath the young Uriah had arrogantly demanded

"Goliath was encased, from top to toe, in several suits of armor, and David did not know how to remove them and cut off the head of the giant.... Uriah the Hittite offered him his services, but under the condition that David secure him an Israelitish wife. David accepted the condition...."
(Unknown Midrash, quoted by R. Moses Al-Sheikh, Legends of the Jews, IV)

of David a Hebrew wife for having helped David remove Goliath's helmet (to enable him to decapitate the giant's head to show it, in victory, to all of Israel)? And maybe he showed vengeance toward Uriah who, he felt, had detracted from his conquest of Goliath in having been needed to help, thus, declare his victory to Israel.

Either way, I, Nathan, had surely suborned the King's "arrogance" that he could survive a test he surely procured directly from God—the very night after I gave him the "belief" of a prophet that God was truly behind him in all he desired. And only now with fresh dirt encasing his baby's body does he finally realize that I am only a prophet of doom, not of hopefulness! The poetry he spoke this morning after he washed and anointed himself, and ate the meal of a mourner—that, finally, his baby would not return—was final proof that while I could predict the death of a baby, I could be counted on for nothing more.

And on this horrible day in the life of a sinner I wouldn't seek to persuade him of anything else. The baby he seemed to care about so little when Bathsheba's Uriah still lived and breathed, seemed, today, at the infant's gravesite, to be the King's whole world. And as the herald of his death, I concealed myself on the outskirts of the cemetery, lest I be a sordid reminder to the King (and to myself) of my deathly role in all of this. In a way I took upon myself the custom of the priests who would stand away seeking to be insulated from the funeral procession, lest I be tainted by the impurity of what that place and moment represented. (I will never come to know if he will have shared my deathly prophecy with Bathsheba.)

12
Through Nathan's Eyes

King David answered, "Summon Bathsheba to me." So she came into the king's presence, and stood before the king. The king swore, saying, "As the LORD lives, who has saved my life from every adversity, as I swore to you by the LORD, the God of Israel, 'Your son Solomon shall succeed me as king, and he shall sit on my throne in my place,' so will I do this day." Then Bathsheba bowed with her face to the ground, and did obeisance to the king, and said, "May my lord King David live forever!" (1 Kings 1:28–31)

When David's time to die drew near, he charged his son Solomon, saying: "I am about to go the way of all the earth. Be strong, be courageous, and keep the charge of the LORD your God, walking in his ways and keeping his statutes, his commandments, his ordinances, and his testimonies, as it is written in the law of Moses, so that you may prosper in all that you do and wherever you turn. Then the LORD will establish his word that he spoke concerning me: 'If your heirs take heed to their way, to walk before me in faithfulness with all their heart and with all their soul, there shall not fail you a successor on the throne of Israel.'" (1 Kings 2:1–4)

I was dazed during my walk to my home from the gravesite. I aimlessly wandered in circles, as had the Children of Israel in the desert, trying to come to terms, as did they, with the mystery of God's Plan for the sinner man. I would say my prayers, and wash my hands and eat the mourner's meal alone—not wishing, for both our sakes, to be in the King's company. As a prophet of bad omen I would remain in my aloneness. And in my aloneness I wondered whether David's sins will have caused a delay in the arrival of the Messiah.

"The crowds that went ahead of him and that followed were shouting, 'Hosanna to the Son of David! Blessed is the one who comes in the name of the Lord! Hosanna in the highest heaven!'" (Matthew 21:9)

I recited, sometimes chanted, from memory, uplifting psalms David had authored to help me deal with my personal pain—as if my own pain was at issue this day. The psalms were beautiful, and I wondered about the complexity of David's makeup—how a man who could have committed the deadly sins that brought us to that gravesite could have authored them. I found no answers!

I have, now, come to know the entire psalm that the King had begun to compose as I left the Palace a week ago. The psalm, blissfully poetic as are all his works, contains no reference to the God-defying incidents that inspired it, to remind all of Israel of David's sin (and that he did not acknowledge it on his own).

The sins of most committed in privacy are known to God, but not all of Israel. Not so, as exemplified by David, are the sins of those who are anointed by God, or appointed to be his anointees. Perhaps David, himself, before he goes to his Maker, will author an introduction to the psalm to explain to Israel its

"It is I, Jesus, who sent my angel to you with this testimony for the churches. I am the root and the descendant of David, the bright morning star."
(Revelation 22:16)

genesis—itself an act of penance that will increase, or perhaps decrease, the love that Israel holds for him.

But as the nighttime approaches, I wonder about my own role in all of this, and the role of prophecy. In describing to him some of the bleak future that lay before David, both in his lifetime and thereafter, I offered no ability to right his wrongs, and possessed none. All I imparted was the ability to reject my parable, or to acknowledge that he was the loathsome "rich man" I had described.

The challenges of today will not leave me. And I will go on. Curiously, David's life was spared for his contrition when, as of that moment I told him his own fate, all that he had done was utter simple words. Words, to many, are easy to speak. But to save his life, the King seemed to need to do little more than to utter them to bring himself away from the precipice. Gratefully, the "deadly" sins that the King committed will not disqualify him from God's grace—forerunner of "The Anointed."

One will always wonder why God allowed the baby to be born from the mortal sin of David and Bathsheba—why He would let an innocent baby be born only to let him die. Perhaps punishment must be that harsh to be punishment, for if the baby had not been born, hard as it might have been for Bathsheba, David would not have suffered in like kind. We must recognize that no prophet will ever shed light on such troubling questions. All prophets, and every man, will be pleased by God's willingness to forgive the seemingly unforgivable, but still plagued by His decisions to take, when He chooses, the upright or blameless. It is the Mystery of God that we shall all pursue, but without answer.

My role in life is not to explore the Mystery, except through the portal of David. Had David denied to me, and to himself, his sin, or hesitated in accepting its reality that turning-point moment one week ago, his Davidic mission would have ended. Had I failed as "the rebuker" of the King who fore-runs the Messiah, he would have "abdicated" the throne that holds his destiny.

My task, then, was not just that of a prophet who foretold the future, but to encourage the accused to recognize the reality that his blood-stained future was fitting for him. A man like David, whose sword will have shed blood as no other has, and a man wantonly willing to kill for love, will have accepted better than others the worthiness of such punishment—even if more peaceful men might not. Those who live by the sword will suffer from it too. And, even though I might have petitioned God to relent on what the future holds for the sons of David, the role God selected for me as David's prosecutor left me unable to do so— even now. Under the Law of Moses, *"the prosecutor cannot be the defender."*

My dual roles of prophet and accuser will have been my role in life. Unlike other men who receive visions from God, my visions do not describe the future of Israel or the world, except

"Now while the Pharisees were gathered together, Jesus asked them this question: 'What do you think of the Messiah? Whose son is he?' They said to him, 'The son of David.' He said to them, 'How is it then that David by the Spirit calls him Lord, saying, "The Lord said to my Lord, 'Sit at my right hand, until I put your enemies under your feet'"? If David thus calls him Lord, how can he be his son?'" (Matthew 22:41–45)

through the prism of David and his House. I will not have remonstrated with the Children of Israel as did Moses or will Isaiah and Jeremiah, nor tell them their good fortune if they follow the Ways of God. I will simply have told the King his lot for his actions, good and bad. And those words will be the reasons for my life. No regret.

There will someday be a book, "The Book of Nathan,"[1] that describes my role in the world; for reasons unclear, it will be lost to Israel in the course of time. But, in truth, there will be no great loss in that. Some men are brought into the world for barely a few moments of worth; for some they are only moments of encounter with disappointment and tragedy. Many, because of my two solitary visits to the King, will see my life, in a Book of Samuel, that way. And as I travel until my own finality, there will be times that, briefly, I will be disillusioned—my finger pressed against the King's chest, telling him that death will never leave his Palace, or that he could not fulfill his dream to build the House of God.

But I will not see my life with disillusion, despite the torment I will have seen on the face of the King and in my looking

"Now the acts of King David, from first to last, are written in the records of the seer Samuel, and in the records of the prophet Nathan, and in the records of the seer Gad...." (1 Chronicles 29:29)

glass. Rather, over all, I will see myself as imparting to the House of Israel the Divine serenity that, despite the waywardness of man, God's infinite grace will always be there to uplift even the sinner. There is no finer exemplar than the story of David. And that will always be the glory of David's checkered life— and my role as God's instrumentality in helping

---

1. 1 Chronicles 29:29.

him to achieve it, albeit through painful words I had to present to him.

No matter what ill I have painted for his future, God will never place more hopeful words on the lips of any man than those I have already told the King of Israel—*and all of Israel:*

When your days are fulfilled and you lie down with your ancestors, I will raise up your offspring after you, who shall come forth from your body, and I will establish his kingdom. He shall build a house for my name, and I will establish the throne of his kingdom forever. I will be a father to him, and he shall be a son to me. When he commits iniquity, I will punish him with a rod such as mortals use, with blows inflicted by human beings. But I will not take my steadfast love from him, as I took it from Saul, whom I put away from before you. Your house and your kingdom shall be made sure forever before me; your throne shall be established forever. (2 Samuel 7:12–16)

"Then those who went ahead and those who followed were shouting, 'Hosanna! Blessed is the one who comes in the name of the Lord! Blessed is the coming kingdom of our ancestor David! Hosanna in the highest heaven!'" (Mark 11:9–10)

"While Jesus was teaching in the temple, he said, 'How can the scribes say that the Messiah is the son of David? David himself, by the Holy Spirit, declared, "The Lord said to my Lord, 'Sit at my right hand, until I put your enemies under your feet.'"'" (Mark 12:35–36)

I will be a father to him, and he shall be a son to me"—words certain to illuminate the House of Israel's understanding of God's relationship to David, forebear of the Messiah.

"David the King of Israel is alive and vigorous." (Rosh Ha-Shanah 25a)

"And now, you will conceive in your womb and bear a son, and you will name him Jesus. He will be great, and will be called the Son of the Most High, and the Lord God will give to him the throne of his ancestor David." (Luke 1:31–32)

On his deathbed Bathsheba will sit beside King David. He will assure her that their son Solomon, born and destined to build the Holy Temple, will reign after him. She will bow her face to the ground, prostrated to the King, and say: *"May my lord King David live forever."*[2]

And so he will!

---

2. 1 Kings 1:31.

ADDITIONAL SOURCES REFLECTING ON THE LIFE OF DAVID IN THE TRADITIONS OF JUDAISM AND CHRISTIANITY

OLD TESTAMENT SOURCES

Psalms 2, 45, 89, and 110, according to tradition authored by
David, speak of the Messiah

Psalm 2

Why do the nations conspire,
    and the peoples plot in vain?
The kings of the earth set themselves,
    and the rulers take counsel together,
    against the Lord and his anointed, saying,
"Let us burst their bonds asunder,
    and cast their cords from us."

He who sits in the heavens laughs;
    the Lord has them in derision.
Then he will speak to them in his wrath,
    and terrify them in his fury, saying,
"I have set my king on Zion, my holy hill."

I will tell of the decree of the Lord:
He said to me, "You are my son;
    today I have begotten you.
Ask of me, and I will make the nations your heritage,
    and the ends of the earth your possession.
You shall break them with a rod of iron,
    and dash them in pieces like a potter's vessel."

Now therefore, O kings, be wise;
    be warned, O rulers of the earth.
Serve the LORD with fear,
    with trembling kiss his feet,
or he will be angry, and you will perish in the way;
    for his wrath is quickly kindled.
Happy are all who take refuge in him.

Psalm 45

My heart overflows with a goodly theme;
    I address my verses to the king;
    my tongue is like the pen of a ready scribe.

You are the most handsome of men;
    grace is poured upon your lips;
    therefore God has blessed you forever.
Gird your sword on your thigh, O mighty one,
    in your glory and majesty.

In your majesty ride on victoriously
    for the cause of truth and to defend the right;
    let your right hand teach you dread deeds.
Your arrows are sharp
    in the heart of the king's enemies;
    the peoples fall under you.

Your throne, O God, endures forever and ever.
    Your royal scepter is a scepter of equity;
    you love righteousness and hate wickedness.

Therefore God, your God, has anointed you
 with the oil of gladness beyond your companions;
 your robes are all fragrant with myrrh and aloes and cassia.
From ivory palaces stringed instruments make you glad;
 daughters of kings are among your ladies of honor;
 at your right hand stands the queen in gold of Ophir.

Hear, O daughter, consider and incline your ear;
 forget your people and your father's house,
 and the king will desire your beauty.
Since he is your lord, bow to him;
 the people of Tyre will seek your favor with gifts,
 the richest of the people with all kinds of wealth.

The princess is decked in her chamber with gold-woven robes;
 in many-colored robes she is led to the king;
 behind her the virgins, her companions, follow.
With joy and gladness they are led along
 as they enter the palace of the king.

In the place of ancestors you, O king, shall have sons;
 you will make them princes in all the earth.
I will cause your name to be celebrated in all generations;
 therefore the peoples will praise you forever and ever.

Psalm 89

I will sing of your steadfast love, O LORD, forever;
 with my mouth I will proclaim your faithfulness to
  all generations.

I declare that your steadfast love is established forever;
    your faithfulness is as firm as the heavens.

You said, "I have made a covenant with my chosen one,
    I have sworn to my servant David:
'I will establish your descendants forever,
    and build your throne for all generations.'"
      Se'lah

Let the heavens praise your wonders, O LORD,
    your faithfulness in the assembly of the holy ones.
For who in the skies can be compared to the LORD?
    Who among the heavenly beings is like the LORD,
a God feared in the council of the holy ones,
    great and awesome above all that are around him?
O LORD God of hosts,
    who is as mighty as you, O LORD?
    Your faithfulness surrounds you.
You rule the raging of the sea;
    when its waves rise, you still them.
You crushed Rahab like a carcass;
    you scattered your enemies with your mighty arm.
The heavens are yours, the earth also is yours;
    the world and all that is in it—you have founded them.
The north and the south—you created them;
    Tabor and Hermon joyously praise your name.
You have a mighty arm;
    strong is your hand, high your right hand.
Righteousness and justice are the foundation of your throne;
    steadfast love and faithfulness go before you.

Happy are the people who know the festal shout,
    who walk, O LORD, in the light of your countenance;
they exult in your name all day long,
    and extol your righteousness.
For you are the glory of their strength;
    by your favor our horn is exalted.
For our shield belongs to the LORD,
    our king to the Holy One of Israel.

Then you spoke in a vision to your faithful one, and said:
    "I have set the crown on one who is mighty,
    I have exalted one chosen from the people.
I have found my servant David;
    with my holy oil I have anointed him;
my hand shall always remain with him;
    my arm also shall strengthen him.
The enemy shall not outwit him,
    the wicked shall not humble him.
I will crush his foes before him
    and strike down those who hate him.
My faithfulness and steadfast love shall be with him;
    and in my name his horn shall be exalted.
I will set his hand on the sea
    and his right hand on the rivers.
He shall cry to me, 'You are my Father,
    my God, and the Rock of my salvation!'
I will make him the firstborn,
    the highest of the kings of the earth.
Forever I will keep my steadfast love for him,
    and my covenant with him will stand firm.

I will establish his line forever,
    and his throne as long as the heavens endure.
If his children forsake my law
    and do not walk according to my ordinances,
if they violate my statutes
    and do not keep my commandments,
then I will punish their transgression with the rod
    and their iniquity with scourges;
but I will not remove from him my steadfast love,
    or be false to my faithfulness.
I will not violate my covenant,
    or alter the word that went forth from my lips.
Once and for all I have sworn by my holiness;
    I will not lie to David.
His line shall continue forever,
    and his throne endure before me like the sun.
It shall be established forever like the moon,
    an enduring witness in the skies."
      Se'lah

But now you have spurned and rejected him;
    you are full of wrath against your anointed.
You have renounced the covenant with your servant;
    you have defiled his crown in the dust.
You have broken through all his walls;
    you have laid his strongholds in ruins.
All who pass by plunder him;
    he has become the scorn of his neighbors.
You have exalted the right hand of his foes;
    you have made all his enemies rejoice.

Moreover, you have turned back the edge of his sword,
    and you have not supported him in battle.
You have removed the scepter from his hand,
    and hurled his throne to the ground.
You have cut short the days of his youth;
    you have covered him with shame.
        Se'lah

How long, O Lord? Will you hide yourself forever?
    How long will your wrath burn like fire?
Remember how short my time is—
    for what vanity you have created all mortals!
Who can live and never see death?
    Who can escape the power of Sheol?
        Se'lah

Lord, where is your steadfast love of old,
    which by your faithfulness you swore to David?
Remember, O Lord, how your servant is taunted;
    how I bear in my bosom the insults of the peoples,
with which your enemies taunt, O Lord,
    with which they taunted the footsteps of your anointed.

Blessed be the Lord forever. Amen and Amen.

Psalm 110

The Lord says to my lord,
    "Sit at my right hand
until I make your enemies your footstool."

The LORD sends out from Zion
> your mighty scepter.
> Rule in the midst of your foes.
Your people will offer themselves willingly
> on the day you lead your forces
> on the holy mountains.
From the womb of the morning,
> like dew, your youth will come to you.
The LORD has sworn and will not change his mind,
> "You are a priest forever according to the order of
> Melchizedek."

The LORD is at your right hand;
> he will shatter kings on the day of his wrath.
He will execute judgment among the nations,
> filling them with corpses;
he will shatter heads
> over the wide earth.
He will drink from the stream by the path;
> therefore he will lift up his head.

1 Kings 1

King David was old and advanced in years; and although they covered him with clothes, he could not get warm. So his servants said to him, "Let a young virgin be sought for my lord the king, and let her wait on the king, and be his attendant; let her lie in your bosom, so that my lord the king may be warm." So they searched for a beautiful girl throughout all the territory of Israel, and found Abishag the Shunammite, and brought her to the king.

The girl was very beautiful. She became the king's attendant and served him, but the king did not know her sexually.

Now Adonijah son of Haggith exalted himself, saying, "I will be king"; he prepared for himself chariots and horsemen, and fifty men to run before him. His father had never at any time displeased him by asking, "Why have you done thus and so?" He was also a very handsome man, and he was born next after Absalom. He conferred with Joab son of Zeruiah and with the priest Abiathar, and they supported Adonijah. But the priest Zadok, and Benaiah son of Jehoiada, and the prophet Nathan, and Shimei, and Rei, and David's own warriors did not side with Adonijah.

Adonijah sacrificed sheep, oxen, and fatted cattle by the stone Zoheleth, which is beside En-rogel, and he invited all his brothers, the king's sons, and all the royal officials of Judah, but he did not invite the prophet Nathan or Benaiah or the warriors or his brother Solomon.

Then Nathan said to Bathsheba, Solomon's mother, "Have you not heard that Adonijah son of Haggith has become king and our lord David does not know it? Now therefore come, let me give you advice, so that you may save your own life and the life of your son Solomon. Go in at once to King David, and say to him, 'Did you not, my lord the king, swear to your servant, saying: Your son Solomon shall succeed me as king, and he shall sit on my throne? Why then is Adonijah king?' Then while you are still there speaking with the king, I will come in after you and confirm your words."

So Bathsheba went to the king in his room. The king was very old; Abishag the Shunammite was attending the king. Bathsheba bowed and did obeisance to the king, and the king said, "What do you wish?" She said to him, "My lord, you swore to your servant by the LORD your God, saying: Your son Solomon shall succeed me as king, and he shall sit on my throne. But now suddenly Adonijah has become king, though you, my lord the king, do not know it. He has sacrificed oxen, fatted cattle, and sheep in abundance, and has invited all the children of the king, the priest Abiathar, and Joab the commander of the army; but your servant Solomon he has not invited. But you, my lord the king—the eyes of all Israel are on you to tell them who shall sit on the throne of my lord the king after him. Otherwise it will come to pass, when my lord the king sleeps with his ancestors, that my son Solomon and I will be counted offenders."

While she was still speaking with the king, the prophet Nathan came in. The king was told, "Here is the prophet Nathan." When he came in before the king, he did obeisance to the king, with his face to the ground. Nathan said, "My lord the king, have you said, 'Adonijah shall succeed me as king, and he shall sit on my throne'? For today he has gone down and has sacrificed oxen, fatted cattle, and sheep in abundance, and has invited all the king's children, Joab the commander of the army, and the priest Abiathar, who are now eating and drinking before him, and saying, 'Long live King Adonijah!' But he did not invite me, your servant, and the priest Zadok, and Benaiah son of Jehoiada, and your servant Solomon. Has this thing been brought about by my lord the king and you have not let your servants know who should sit on the throne of my lord the king after him?"

King David answered, "Summon Bathsheba to me." So she came into the king's presence, and stood before the king. The king swore, saying, "As the LORD lives, who has saved my life from every adversity, as I swore to you by the LORD, the God of Israel, 'Your son Solomon shall succeed me as king, and he shall sit on my throne in my place,' so will I do this day." Then Bathsheba bowed with her face to the ground, and did obeisance to the king, and said, "May my lord King David live forever!"

King David said, "Summon to me the priest Zadok, the prophet Nathan, and Benaiah son of Jehoiada." When they came before the king, the king said to them, "Take with you the servants of your lord, and have my son Solomon ride on my own mule, and bring him down to Gihon. There let the priest Zadok and the prophet Nathan anoint him king over Israel; then blow the trumpet, and say, 'Long live King Solomon!' You shall go up following him. Let him enter and sit on my throne; he shall be king in my place; for I have appointed him to be ruler over Israel and over Judah." Benaiah son of Jehoiada answered the king, "Amen! May the LORD, the God of my lord the king, so ordain. As the LORD has been with my lord the king, so may he be with Solomon, and make his throne greater than the throne of my lord King David."

So the priest Zadok, the prophet Nathan, and Benaiah son of Jehoiada, and the Cherethites and the Pelethites, went down and had Solomon ride on King David's mule, and led him to Gihon. There the priest Zadok took the horn of oil from the tent and anointed Solomon. Then they blew the trumpet, and all the people said, "Long live King Solomon!" And all the people went up following him, playing on pipes and rejoicing with great joy, so that the earth quaked at their noise.

Adonijah and all the guests who were with him heard it as they finished feasting. When Joab heard the sound of the trumpet, he said, "Why is the city in an uproar?" While he was still speaking, Jonathan son of the priest Abiathar arrived. Adonijah said, "Come in, for you are a worthy man and surely you bring good news." Jonathan answered Adonijah, "No, for our lord King David has made Solomon king; the king has sent with him the priest Zadok, the prophet Nathan, and Benaiah son of Jehoiada, and the Cherethites and the Pelethites; and they had him ride on the king's mule; the priest Zadok and the prophet Nathan have anointed him king at Gihon; and they have gone up from there rejoicing, so that the city is in an uproar. This is the noise that you heard. Solomon now sits on the royal throne. Moreover the king's servants came to congratulate our lord King David, saying, 'May God make the name of Solomon more famous than yours, and make his throne greater than your throne.' The king bowed in worship on the bed and went on to pray thus, 'Blessed be the LORD, the God of Israel, who today has granted one of my offspring to sit on my throne and permitted me to witness it.'"

Then all the guests of Adonijah got up trembling and went their own ways. Adonijah, fearing Solomon, got up and went to grasp the horns of the altar. Solomon was informed, "Adonijah is afraid of King Solomon; see, he has laid hold of the horns of the altar, saying, 'Let King Solomon swear to me first that he will not kill his servant with the sword.'" So Solomon responded, "If he proves to be a worthy man, not one of his hairs shall fall to the ground; but if wickedness is found in him, he shall die." Then King Solomon sent to have him brought down from the altar. He came to do obeisance to King Solomon; and Solomon said to him, "Go home."

Hosea 3

The LORD said to me again, "Go, love a woman who has a lover and is an adulteress, just as the LORD loves the people of Israel, though they turn to other gods and love raisin cakes." So I bought her for fifteen shekels of silver and a homer of barley and a measure of wine. And I said to her, "You must remain as mine for many days; you shall not play the whore, you shall not have intercourse with a man, nor I with you." For the Israelites shall remain many days without king or prince, without sacrifice or pillar, without ephod or teraphim. Afterward the Israelites shall return and seek the LORD their God, and David their king; they shall come in awe to the LORD and to his goodness in the latter days.

Jeremiah 30:1–9

The word that came to Jeremiah from the LORD: Thus says the LORD, the God of Israel: Write in a book all the words that I have spoken to you. For the days are surely coming, says the LORD, when I will restore the fortunes of my people, Israel and Judah, says the LORD, and I will bring them back to the land that I gave to their ancestors and they shall take possession of it. These are the words that the LORD spoke concerning Israel and Judah: Thus says the LORD: We have heard a cry of panic, of terror, and no peace. Ask now, and see, can a man bear a child? Why then do I see every man with his hands on his loins like a woman in labor? Why has every face turned pale? Alas! that day is so great there is none like it; it is a time of distress for Jacob; yet he shall be rescued from it. On that day, says the LORD of hosts, I will break the yoke from off his neck, and I will burst his bonds, and strangers shall no more make a servant of him. But they shall serve the LORD their God and David their king, whom I will raise up for them.

1 Chronicles 17

Now when David settled in his house, David said to the prophet Nathan, "I am living in a house of cedar, but the ark of the covenant of the LORD is under a tent." Nathan said to David, "Do all that you have in mind, for God is with you."

But that same night the word of the LORD came to Nathan, saying: Go and tell my servant David: Thus says the LORD: You shall not build me a house to live in. For I have not lived in a house since the day I brought out Israel to this very day, but I have lived in a tent and a tabernacle. Wherever I have moved about among all Israel, did I ever speak a word with any of the judges of Israel, whom I commanded to shepherd my people, saying, Why have you not built me a house of cedar? Now therefore thus you shall say to my servant David: Thus says the LORD of hosts: I took you from the pasture, from following the sheep, to be ruler over my people Israel; and I have been with you wherever you went, and have cut off all your enemies before you; and I will make for you a name, like the name of the great ones of the earth. I will appoint a place for my people Israel, and will plant them, so that they may live in their own place, and be disturbed no more; and evildoers shall wear them down no more, as they did formerly, from the time that I appointed judges over my people Israel; and I will subdue all your enemies.

Moreover I declare to you that the LORD will build you a house. When your days are fulfilled to go to be with your ancestors, I will raise up your offspring after you, one of your own sons, and I will establish his kingdom. He shall build a house for me, and I will establish his throne forever. I will be a father to him, and he shall be a son to me. I will not take my steadfast love from him, as I took it from him who was before you, but I will confirm him in my house and in my kingdom forever, and his throne shall be established forever. In accordance with all these words and all this vision, Nathan spoke to David.

Then King David went in and sat before the LORD, and said, "Who am I, O LORD God, and what is my house, that you have brought me thus far? And even this was a small thing in your sight, O God; you have also spoken of your servant's house for a great while to come. You regard me as someone of high rank, O LORD God! And what more can David say to you for honoring your servant? You know your servant. For your servant's sake, O LORD, and according to your own heart, you have done all these great deeds, making known all these great things. There is no one like you, O LORD, and there is no God besides you, according to all that we have heard with our ears. Who is like your people Israel, one nation on the earth whom God went to redeem to be his people, making for yourself a name for great and terrible things, in driving out nations before your people whom you redeemed from Egypt? And you made your people Israel to be your people forever; and you, O LORD, became their God.

"And now, O LORD, as for the word that you have spoken concerning your servant and concerning his house, let it be established forever, and do as you have promised. Thus your name will be established and magnified forever in the saying, 'The LORD of hosts, the God of Israel, is Israel's God'; and the house of your servant David will be established in your presence. For you, my God, have revealed to your servant that you will build a house for him; therefore your servant has found it possible to pray before you. And now, O LORD, you are God, and you have promised this good thing to your servant; therefore may it please you to bless the house of your servant, that it may continue forever before you. For you, O LORD, have blessed and are blessed forever."

NEW TESTAMENT SOURCES

Revelation 5:1–5

Then I saw in the right hand of the one seated on the throne a scroll written on the inside and on the back, sealed with seven seals; and I saw a mighty angel proclaiming with a loud voice, "Who is worthy to open the scroll and break its seals?" And no one in heaven or on earth or under the earth was able to open the scroll or to look into it. And I began to weep bitterly because no one was found worthy to open the scroll or to look into it. Then one of the elders said to me, "Do not weep. See, the Lion of the tribe of Judah, the Root of David, has conquered, so that he can open the scroll and its seven seals."

Romans 1:1–4

Paul, a servant of Jesus Christ, called to be an apostle, set apart for the gospel of God, which he promised beforehand through his prophets in the holy scriptures, the gospel concerning his Son, who was descended from David according to the flesh and was declared to be Son of God with power according to the spirit of holiness by resurrection from the dead, Jesus Christ our Lord....

"LIKE FATHER, LIKE SON TRADITION"

The Legends of the Jews, IV, p. 82
Unknown Midrash quoted by Makiri,
Psalms 118, 124

In spite of his piety, Jesse was not always proof against temptation. One of his slaves caught his fancy and he would have entered into illicit relations with her, had his wife, Naẓbat, the daughter of Adiel, not frustrated the plan. She disguised herself as the slave, and Jesse, deceived by the ruse, met his own wife. The child born by Naẓbat was given out as the son of the freed slave, so that the father might not discover the deception practiced upon him. This child was David.

Legends, IV, p. 82
Unknown Midrash quoted by Makiri,
Psalms 118, 124

Beauty and talent, Adam's gifts to David, did not shield their possessor against hardship. As the supposed son of a slave, he was banished from association with his brothers, and his days were passed in the desert tending his father's sheep. It was his shepherd life that prepared him for his later exalted position. With gentle consideration he led the flocks entrusted to him.

Legends, IV, p. 84

The amazement was great that the son a slave should be made king. Then the wife of Jesse revealed her secret and declared herself the mother of David.

GROWING UP AS A SHEPHERD

Legends, IV, p. 83

In the solitude of the desert David had opportunities of displaying his extraordinary physical strength. One day he slew four lions and three bears, though he had no weapons. His most serious adventure was with the reëm. David encountered the mammoth beast asleep and taking it for a mountain, he began to ascend it. Suddenly the reëm awoke and David found himself high up in the air on its horns. He vowed, if he were rescued, to build a temple to God, one hundred ells in height, as high as the horns of the reëm. Thereupon God sent a lion. The king of the beasts inspired even the reëm with awe. The reëm prostrated himself and David could easily descend from his perch. At that moment, a deer appeared. The lion pursued after him and David was saved from the lion as well as the reëm.

He continued to lead the life of a shepherd until, at the age of twenty-eight, he was anointed king by Samuel, who was taught that the despised youngest son of Jesse was to be king.

"THE ANOINTING"
Legends, IV, p. 84

The election of David was obvious from what happened with the holy oil with which he was anointed. When Samuel had tried to pour the oil on David's brothers, it had remained in the horn, but at David's approach it flowed of its own accord, and poured itself out over him. The drops on his garments changed into diamonds and pearls, and after the act of anointing him, the horn was as full as before.

Legends, VI, p. 249

In anointing David, Samuel used a "horn" filled with oil, but in anointing Saul he took a cruse; the horn was the symbol of David's everlasting kingdom, whereas the cruse represented Saul's temporary rule.

Legends, IV, p. 84

The anointing of David was for a time kept a secret, but its effect appeared in the gift of prophecy which manifested itself in David and in his extraordinary development. His new accomplishments naturally earned envy for him.

THE TEMPLE
Legends, IV, p. 102

But in the very night in which David conceived the plan of building the Temple, God said to Nathan the prophet: "Hasten to David. I know him to be a man with whom execution follows fast upon the heels of thought, and I should not like him to hire laborers for the Temple work and then, disappointed, complain of me. I furthermore know him to be a man who obligates himself by vows to do good deeds and I desire to spare him the embarrassment of having to apply to the Sanhedrin for absolution from his vow."

Mekilta Shirah 1, 34b

The Temple, though built by Solomon, is nevertheless called the house of David because the latter had set his heart upon the building of the Temple; had not God prevented him, he would have carried out his plan.

Legends, IV, pp. 102–3

When David heard Nathan's message for him, he began to tremble and he said: "Ah, verily, God hath found me unworthy to erect His sanctuary." But God replied with these words: "Nay, the blood shed by thee I consider as sacrificial blood, but I do not care to have thee build the Temple, because then it would be eternal and indestructible....I foresee that Israel will commit sins. I shall wreak My wrath upon the Temple, and Israel will be saved from annihilation."

DAVID'S ATONEMENT
Legends, IV, pp. 107–9

All these sufferings did not suffice to atone for David's sin. God once said to him: "How much longer shall this sin be hidden in thy hand and remain unatoned? On thy account the priestly city of Nob was destroyed, on thy account Doeg the Edomite was cast out of the communion of the pious, and on thy account Saul and his three sons were slain. What dost thou desire now—that thy house should perish, or that thou thyself shouldst be delivered into the hands of thine enemies?" David chose the latter doom.

It happened one day when he was hunting. Satan, in the guise of a deer, enticed him further and further, into the very territory of the Philistines, where he was recognized by Ishbi the giant, the brother of Goliath, his adversary. Desirous of avenging his brother, he seized David, and cast him into a winepress, where the king would have suffered a torturous end, if by a miracle the earth beneath him had not begun to sink, and so saved him from instantaneous death. His plight, however, remained desperate, and it required a second miracle to rescue him.

In that hour Abishai, the cousin of David, was preparing for the advent of the Sabbath, for the king's misfortune happened on Friday as the Sabbath was about to come in. When Abishai poured out water to wash himself, he suddenly caught sight of drops of blood in it. Then he was startled by a dove that came to him plucking out her plumes, and moaning and wailing. Abishai exclaimed: "The dove is the symbol of the people of Israel. It cannot be but that David, the king of Israel, is in distress." Not finding the king at home, he was confirmed in his fears, and he determined to go on a search for David on the swiftest animal at his command, the king's own saddle-beast. But first he had to obtain the permission of the sages to mount the animal ridden by the king, for the law forbids a subject to avail himself of things set aside for the personal use of a king.

Only the impending danger could justify the exception made in this case.

Scarcely had Abishai mounted the king's animal, when he found himself in the land of the Philistines, for the earth had contracted miraculously. He met Orpah, the mother of the four giant sons. She was about to kill him, but he anticipated the blow and slew her. Ishbi, seeing that he now had two opponents, stuck his lance into the ground, and hurled David up in the air, in the expectation that when he fell he would be transfixed by the lance. At that moment Abishai appeared, and by pronouncing the Name of God he kept David suspended 'twixt heaven and earth.

Abishai questioned David how such evil plight had overtaken him, and David told him of his conversation with God, and how he himself had chosen to fall into the hands of the enemy, rather than permit the ruin of his house. Abishai replied: "Reverse thy prayer, plead for thyself, and not for thy descendants. Let thy children sell wax, and do thou not afflict thyself about their destiny." The two men joined their prayers, and pleaded with God to avert David's threatening doom. Abishai again uttered the Name of God, and David dropped to earth uninjured. Now both of them ran away swiftly, pursued by Ishbi. When the giant heard of his mother's death, his strength forsook him, and he was slain by David and Abishai.

THE DEATH OF DAVID
Legends, IV, pp. 113–14

David once besought God to tell him when he would die. His petition was not granted, for God has ordained that no man shall foreknow his end. One thing, however, was revealed to David, that his death would occur at the age of seventy on the Sabbath day. David desired that he might be permitted to die on Friday. This wish, too, was denied him, because God said that He delighted more in one day passed by David in the study of the Torah, than in a thousand holocausts offered by Solomon in the Temple. Then David petitioned that life might be vouchsafed him until Sunday; this, too, was refused, because God said it would be an infringement of the rights of Solomon, for one reign may not overlap by a hairbreadth the time assigned to another.

Thereafter David spent every Sabbath exclusively in the study of the Torah, in order to secure himself against the Angel of Death, who has no power to slay a man while he is occupied with the fulfillment of God's commandments. The Angel of Death had to resort to cunning to gain possession of David. One Sabbath day, which happened to be also the Pentecost holiday, the king was absorbed in study, when he heard a sound in the garden. He rose and descended the stairway leading from his palace to the garden, to discover the cause of the noise. No sooner had he set foot on the steps than they tumbled in, and David was killed. The Angel of Death had caused the noise in order to utilize the moment when David should interrupt his study. The king's corpse could not be moved on the Sabbath, which was painful to those with him, as it was lying exposed to the rays of the sun. So Solomon summoned several eagles, and they stood guard over the body, shading it with their outstretched pinions.

DAVID IN PARADISE

Legends, IV, pp. 114–16
[cites omitted]

The death of David did not mean the end of his glory and grandeur. It merely caused a change of scene. In the heavenly realm as on earth David ranks among the first. The crown upon his head outshines all others, and whenever he moves out of Paradise to present himself before God, suns, stars, angels, seraphim, and other holy beings run to meet him. In the heavenly court-room a throne of fire of gigantic dimensions is erected for him directly opposite to the throne of God. Seated on this throne and surrounded by the kings of the house of David and other Israelitish kings, he intones wondrously beautiful psalms. At the end he always cites the verse: "The Lord reigns forever and ever," to which the archangel Metatron and those with him reply: "Holy, holy, holy, is the Lord of hosts!" This is the signal for the holy Hayyot and heaven and earth to join in with praise. Finally the kings of the house of David sing the verse: "And the Lord shall be king over all; in that day shall the Lord be one, and His name one."

The greatest distinction to be accorded David is reserved for the judgment day, when God will prepare a great banquet in Paradise for all the righteous. At David's petition, God Himself will be present at the banquet, and will sit on His throne, opposite to which David's throne will be placed. At the end of the banquet, God will pass the wine cup over which grace is said, to Abraham, with the words: "Pronounce the blessing over the wine, thou who art the father of the pious of the world."

Abraham will reply: "I am not worthy to pronounce the blessing, for I am the father also of the Ishmaelites, who kindle God's wrath." God will then turn to Isaac: "Say the blessing, for thou wert bound upon the altar as a sacrifice." "I am not worthy," he will reply, "for the children of my son Esau destroyed the Temple." Then to Jacob: "Do you speak the blessing, thou whose children were blameless." Jacob also will decline the honor on the ground that he was married to two sisters at the same time, which later was strictly prohibited by the Torah. God will then turn to Moses: "Say the blessing, for thou didst receive the law and didst fulfil its precepts." Moses will answer: "I am not worthy to do it, seeing that I was not found worthy to enter the Holy Land." God will next offer the honor to Joshua, who both led Israel into the Holy Land, and fulfilled the commandments of the law. He, too, will refuse to pronounce the blessing, because he was not found worthy to bring forth a son. Finally God will turn to David with the words: "Take the cup and say the blessing, thou the sweetest singer in Israel and Israel's king." And David will reply: "Yes I will pronounce the blessing, for I am worthy of the honor." Then God will take the Torah and read various passages from it, and David will recite a psalm in which both the pious in Paradise and the wicked in hell will join with a loud Amen. Thereupon God will send his angels to lead the wicked from hell to Paradise.

Legends, VI, p. 272

As early an authority as R. Akiba (Sanhedrin 38b, and parallel passages) speaks of the throne upon which David will sit on the Day of Judgment. There can be no doubt that these legends about David are connected with the view that he is the promised Messiah; see Sanhedrin 98a; Rosh Ha-Shanah 25a which reads: David, the king of Israel, lives for ever; Tehillim 5, 52, 57, 298; 75, 340; 2 ARN 45, 125; Shitah Hadashah 2 (which reads: David is the first and the last of the Jewish rulers); Zohar I 82b; III, 84a. In a kabbalistic rendering (Sanhedrin 98b) in the days to come God will raise "another David" to be the Messiah, whose viceroy will be the first David. See also Mishle 19, 87, where David is given as one of the names of the Messiah. One of David's distinctions which he shares with the three patriarchs, and Moses, Aaron, Miriam, and Benjamin is that his corpse was not touched by worms; Baba Batra 17a; Tehillim 119, 492; Derek Erez Z., I (end). Comp. also Acts 13.36. Baba Batra, loc. cit., states that David is one of the few over whom the evil inclination had no power. Somewhat different is the state of Yerushalmi Sotah 5, 20c: Abraham turned the evil inclination into the good inclination, but David was unable to do that, and he therefore slew the evil inclination. This wishes to convey that David (as repentance for his sin with Bathsheba) denied himself the pleasures which are permitted by the law, and lived like an ascetic, whereas Abraham served God in enjoying life. The world was created for the sake of David; Sanhedrin 98b, where Moses and the Messiah are regarded by some authorities as those for whose sake the world was created. See the similar statement in Berakot 61b, which reads: The world was created only for the very pious or for the extremely wicked; for the former the world to come, and this world for the latter....

In ShR 25.8 Michael is first requested to say the blessing; but with "angelic" modesty passes on this honor to Gabriel, who likewise refuses the honor, and asks the patriarchs to say the blessing. They in turn ask Moses and Aaron, who pass on the honor to the elders, and the latter find David to be the one deserving of this great distinction. In the world to come there will be no company of righteous of which David will not be a member; Shmuel 19, 104.

THE INCIDENT

Legends, IV, p. 104

Furthermore, the Bathsheba episode was a punishment for David's excessive self-consciousness. He had fairly besought God to lead him into temptation, that he might give proof of his constancy. It came about thus: He once complained to God: "O Lord of the world, why do people say God of Abraham, God of Isaac, God of Jacob and why not God of David?" The answer came: "Abraham, Isaac, and Jacob were tried by me, but thou hast not yet been proved." David entreated: "Then examine me, O Lord, and try me." And God said: "I will prove thee, and I shall even grant thee what I did not grant the Patriarchs. I shall tell thee beforehand that thou wilt fall into temptation through a woman."

Sanhedrin 107a;
Tehillim 18, 157; 26, 216

Once Satan appeared to him in the shape of a bird. David threw a dart at him. Instead of striking Satan, it glanced off and broke a wicker screen which hid Bathsheba combing her hair. The sight of her aroused passion in the king.

ER 2, 7

David realized his transgression and for twenty-two years he was a penitent. Daily he wept a whole hour and ate his "bread with ashes."

Legends, IV, p. 104

But he had to undergo still heavier penance. For a half-year he suffered with leprosy, and even the Sanhedrin, which usually was in close personal attendance upon him, had to leave him. He lived not only in physical but also in spiritual isolation, for the Shekinah departed from him during that time.

New Catholic Encyclopedia, IV, p. 658

A shadow is cast over David's life and work by his adultery with Bethsabee and his murder of her husband, Uria the Hethite (2 Sam 11:1–27). Although David confessed his sin (2 Sam 12:1–14), his bad example unleashed the worst passions within his family. Amnon's rape of his half sister Thamar led to his assassination by Absalom (2 Sam 13:1–33) followed by the latter's flight, revolt and death (2 Sam 13:34–18:33). Intrigues of disastrous consequences were carried on for the succession to the throne, which was ultimately gained by Solomon (3 Kgs 1:1–53).

AFTERMATH COMMENTARIES
Kaballah, p. 348

In the kabbalistic commentaries on the Bible many events were explained by such hidden history of the transmigration of various souls which return in a later gilgul to situations similar to those of an earlier state, in order to repair damage which they had previously caused. The early Kabbalah provides the basis of this idea: there Moses and Jethro, for example, are considered the reincarnations of Abel and Cain; David, Bathsheba and Uriah, of Adam, Eve, and the serpent; and Job, of Terah the father of Abraham.

Legends, IV, pp. 104, 105

Of all the punishments, however, inflicted upon David, none was so severe as the rebellion of his own son....The knowledge that a part of Absalom's following sided with him in secret—that though he was pursued by his son, his friends remained true to him—somewhat consoled David in his distress. He thought that in these circumstances, if the worst came to the worst, Absalom would at least feel pity for him.

Legends, VI, pp. 266–67

In the Book of Psalms, the psalm which David composed "when he fled from Absalom" follows the one concerning Gog and Magog (the "nations in uproar against God and the Messiah"; comp. Ps. 2 and 3). The reason is that if one should say: "How is it possible that the slave should rebel against his master?," he will receive the answer: "Behold, it even happened that the son rebelled against the father." See Berakot 10z.

Legends, IV, pp. 105–6

At first, however, the despair of David knew no bounds. He was on the point of worshipping an idol when his friend Hushai the Archite approached him, saying: "The people will wonder that such a king should serve idols." David replied: "Should a king such as I am be killed by his own son? It is better for me to serve idols than that God should be held responsible for my misfortune, and His name thus be desecrated." Hushai reproached him: "Why didst thou marry a captive?" "There is no wrong in that," replied David, "it is permitted according to the law." Thereupon Hushai: "But thou didst disregard the connection between the passage permitting it and the one that follows almost immediately after it in the Scriptures, dealing with the disobedient and rebellious son, the natural issue of such a marriage."

Legends, VI, p. 267

David served an idol because he wished to make his fate appear just in the eyes of men, who say: "Behold, he merited his punishment." That David on this occasion had his head covered and went barefoot (2 Sam 15:30) was due to the fact that the Synedrion excommunicated him (on account of his sin with Bath-sheba?) and one who is excommunicated is forbidden to put on shoes or to have his head uncovered. The ban was removed from him by his master Ira.

OTHER DAVID STORIES
Legends, IV, p. 89

As God stood by David in his duel with Goliath, so he stood by him in many other of his difficulties. Often when he thought all hope lost, the arm of God suddenly succored him, and in unexpected ways, not only bringing relief, but also conveying instruction on God's wise and just guidance of the world.

2 Alphabet of Ben Sira 24b;
Targum Psalm 57.3

On another occasion David expressed his doubt of God's wisdom in having formed such apparently useless creatures as spiders are. They do nothing but spin a web that has no value. He was to have striking proof that even a spider's web may serve an important purpose. On one occasion he had taken refuge in a cave, and Saul and his attendants, in pursuit of him, were about to enter and seek him there. But God sent a spider to weave its web across the opening, and Saul told his men to desist from fruitless search in the cave, for the spider's web was undeniable proof that no one had passed through its entrance.

Glossary

Abimelech. A son of Jerubbaal at the time of Gideon, the most prominent of the Judges of Israel that preceded the period of Kings. In his murderous effort to become King of Shechem he killed the seventy sons of Jerubbaal, except Jotham. Jotham spoke out unsuccessfully against him in a parable, and Abimelech was anointed king by the men of Shechem. After three years of his reign, Shechem rebelled against him and he was killed.

Abraham. The father of monotheism. According to Tradition, his father Terah made idols. When alone in his father's workshop, Abraham broke his father's idols to prove that they had no inherent power. Abraham, his son Isaac, and grandson Jacob were Israel's three patriarchs.

Absalom. David's favorite son ("Would to God I had died for thee, Absalom"). Absalom killed his half-brother Amnon (See **Tamar,** infra). He sought to replace David and waged a rebellion against him. Riding through the brush he was hanged when his long hair was caught on a tree. David's men killed him to David's great personal suffering.

Adam. The first human—created by God from dust. According to Tradition, as a prophet God gave him a vision of the future that showed that a potentially great man, David, would die soon after his birth. Adam successfully asked God to deduct seventy years from his own life and give them to David. David is said to have died on his seventieth birthday.

Adonijah. Son of David who tried unsuccessfully to claim his crown when David was on his deathbed. After David's death, he asked Bathsheba to persuade Solomon to let him have his father's concubine Abishag the Shunammite woman. When Solomon heard that, recognizing it meant that Adonijah sought to reassert himself into the kingship, Solomon had his half-brother killed.

Basherte. Yiddish for "the appointed one." The idea derives from the Talmud (Sanhedrin 22a) which says that "forty days before the gestation of the fetus a Heavenly voice proclaims, 'the daughter of so and so will marry the son of so and so.'" In conventional terms: "one's destiny."

Bathsheba. First married to Uriah the Hittite—a soldier in the King's army, who was sent by David to his death in battle against the Ammonites—she became a wife of David. After her unnamed son born of an adulterous liaison with David died, she bore Solomon, son to David. Solomon built the first Temple.

Book of Chronicles. Chronicles I and II are holy texts in the Tanakh. First Chronicles 29:29 refers to a Book of Nathan, but no such volume survives to appear in the Hebrew Bible, the Christian Bible, or the Apocrypha.

Chatassi L'Adonai. Hebrew for "I have sinned against God." These are the words David is extolled for having said to Nathan without attempting to mitigate his offenses of adultery and murder (2 Samuel 12:13).

Dovid Hamelech. Hebrew for "King David."

Dvar Torah. "A Word of Torah." In Jewish Tradition, lasting until today, observant individuals, out of respect for God, will frequently discuss a brief interpretation of the Bible or Talmud when sharing a meal or encounter.

Goliath. The Philistine giant who taunted Israel at the time of King Saul. David, still a boy, came forward to do battle against the giant and promptly killed him with a slingshot, earning him the admiration of the throngs, and jealousy of King Saul, whom he later succeeded as King.

Good Samaritan. A parable told by Jesus, described in the Gospel of Luke, where the Priests and Levites are condemned for "crossing to the other side of the road" and hastening to their chores in the Temple rather than helping a sick man lying near death on the road.

Isaiah. Famous Prophet of Israel before and during the period of the destruction of the First Temple. Among his other rebukes, Isaiah used a parable to compare the Children of Israel to a vineyard that a man treasured but that constantly produced poor grapes, after which he destroyed it.

Jeremiah. An ancient rebuking prophet of Judah discussed at length in the Book of Jeremiah. He was imprisoned by the King Zedekiah of Judah when Jeremiah prophesied that God was going to hand Jerusalem over to the King of Babylonia.

Joab. A general and King David's chief of staff. When David wanted to have Uriah killed for his refusal to return to his wife Bathsheba, David placed a sealed death warrant in the hands of Uriah, directing him to give it to Joab at the battlefront. Joab carried out the King's order—he dispatched

Uriah to the frontlines of the fiercest battle and directed his troops to withdraw from Uriah so that he would be killed by the enemy, which occurred.

Jotham. One of the seventy sons of Jerubbaal at the time of the famous Judge Gideon. See *Abimelech,* supra.

Maacah. Daughter of Talmai, King of Geshur. She was taken in battle by David as an *eishat yi'fat toar,* a beautiful woman, which was the victor's "right" in battle. David married her, and she later gave birth to his son Absalom and daughter Tamar.

Michal. A wife of David, daughter of King Saul. Saul, in jealousy over David, took her from David and gave her to another man, Palti. Later, returned to David, she became displeased with David, now the King, following his celebrating with the Holy Ark. She remonstrated with him for having been so unrestrained in the presence of his subjects.

Moses. God's greatest servant who took the Hebrews out of slavery in Egypt and later received the Torah directly from God at Mount Sinai. According to Tradition, after he was born his sister, Miriam, watched over him when he lay in a basket on the Nile to hide him from Pharaoh's death decree for Hebrew firstborns. Even as a young girl, Miriam was a prophetess who spread word that Moses would become the Redeemer.

Nathan. A prophet—meaning someone who communes directly with God—who lived at the time of King David. Three incidents involving him appear in 2 Samuel:. (1) When David told Nathan he wanted to build the Temple, God came to Nathan instructing him to tell David that it would not be so. (2) When God was angry at David for his conduct relating to Bathsheba and Uriah, he dispatched Nathan to confront David. (3) When Nathan learned that Adonijah, another son of David, was presenting himself as David's successor, Nathan reported this to Bathsheba. The two went to David, on his deathbed, who assured her that her son Solomon would reign after him. According to some traditions, Nathan wrote at least part of 2 Samuel.

Philistines. The blood enemy of the Hebrews at the time of King Saul.

Samuel. A prophet of God at the time of King Saul and King David. He was born to Elkanah and Hannah, who had been barren. Disheartened by her barren state, she went to the House of Priests and swore to the High Priest Eli that if she conceived a child he would follow the way of ascetic Nazirites. She soon gave birth to Samuel. Later, when Israel asked that God anoint a king, Samuel tried unsuccessfully to persuade God not to.

Saul. First King of Israel, succeeded by David when God became disenchanted with him—Saul failed to follow God's command to destroy the tribe of Amalek. Samuel told Saul that God would choose as his successor—"a man after His own heart"—David. Saul was the father of David's first wife Michal and Jonathan, David's great friend.

Solomon. Son of King David and Bathsheba. He succeeded David as King and built the First Temple. Widely known for his great wisdom, he was the author of, among other Holy Writings, Ecclesiastes and the Song of Songs.

Tamar. Daughter of David and sister of Absalom. When her half-brother Amnon lured her to his chamber feigning illness and then seduced and raped her, Absalom arranged to have Amnon killed.

T'shuvah. Hebrew for "repentance." In Tradition, David is considered a paradigm for repentance or contrition in the manner in which he acted when confronted with his sins by the Prophet Nathan.

Uriah. A Hittite soldier and husband of Bathsheba, later wife of David. He was killed by the Ammonites when David directed Joab that Uriah be sent to the fiercest battle against that enemy of Israel. According to Tradition, when David slayed Goliath, but wasn't able to remove the giant's helmet so that David could place Goliath's head on a stake, Uriah offered to help David. He conditioned it on David's promise that he could marry a Hebrew woman. That woman would be Bathsheba. When Bathsheba later became pregnant with David's son, Uriah (unaware of the adultery) refused to return to his wife's bed, stating that his comrades-in-arms were still at risk at the battlefront.